'I don't want to dance with you,' Jillian said.

'Tough.' On the crowded dance floor, Drake Cullinane swayed slowly, holding her to him with one warm hand against her exposed skin.

'Cullinane—' She held herself stiffly, fighting his draw.

'Shh…it's a good song.' His warm breath ruffled the hair at her temple. She wondered if he knew that his index finger stroked slowly between the silk and her skin.

Of course he knew. This man missed nothing.

For just a moment she forgot that he was her enemy. Their gazes met, the smoke from his grey eyes curling deep inside her.

Then grey hardened to steel, as if he'd shaken off a dream. Jillian felt him tense and she jerked back, anger surging as she remembered who he was, what he represented.

Confusion filled her that for even one moment she could forget why she was here.

Dear Reader

Welcome to this month's fantastic line-up from Special Edition™. In *Older, Wiser...Pregnant*, the latest THAT'S MY BABY! title, Laurel Cameron returns to her home town and her first love, but will Beau Walker accept her when he finds out she's carrying another man's child?

Meanwhile, Travis Winchester is in big trouble in Pamela Toth's *The Mail-Order Mix-Up*, he's met the woman of his dreams, but she's his *brother's* mail-order bride! And don't miss the latest instalment of Victoria Pade's A RANCHING FAMILY series, where Yance Culhane unexpectedly finds an instant family.

Cathy Gillen Thacker's back this month, too, with the second in her trilogy and an absolute delight! An unlikely couple turn up the heat, oblivious to the blizzard raging outside their door...

Finally this month, will love conquer all? Find out in *Meant To Be Married* where lovers have to contend with their families' ill-will before they can wed. And it's a case of opposites attract when Jillian Marshall decides to become *The Bodyguard's Bride*.

Happy reading

The Editors.

The Bodyguard's Bride

JEAN BRASHEAR

SILHOUETTE

SPECIAL EDITION®

Silhouette, Silhouette Special Edition and Colophon are registered trademarks of Harlequin Books S.A., used under licence.

First published in Great Britain 1999
Silhouette Books, Eton House, 18-24 Paradise Road,
Richmond, Surrey TW9 1SR

© Jean Brashear 1998

ISBN 0 373 24206 9

23-9905

Printed and bound in Spain
by Litografia Rosés S.A., Barcelona

JEAN BRASHEAR

A letter to Rod Stewart resulting in a Cinderella birthday for her daughter sowed the seeds of Jean Brashear's writing career. For a woman still deeply in love with her husband after twenty-eight years and who has two fascinating children, writing romance is a natural turn. It's her goal to give today's readers—juggling diverse responsibilities—stories that will recharge the batteries, warm the heart and fire the imagination with the message dearest to her: Love has the power to change the world...and is the magic that can make any life a great adventure.

AN INTERVIEW WITH *Jean Brashear*

What was your inspiration for THE BODYGUARD'S BRIDE?

JB: 'The image that spurred this book's creation was one of a man so deep under cover, so far inside the enemy's boundaries that he's hanging on through sheer will and a powerful sense of duty. Then I thought how interesting it would be, just as his operation reaches the most dangerous point, to introduce a woman who's every bit as determined and duty-bound and who could spell disaster to his operation.'

What about the Special Edition™ line appeals to you as a reader and as a writer?

JB: 'My book possesses what I think of as hallmarks of the line—powerful emotion and a strong sense of family. I love nothing better than getting deep into characters' lives, whether I'm reading them or writing them, and feeling every emotion as though it were my own.'

Why is THE BODYGUARD'S BRIDE special to you?

JB: 'Because it's a story of two strong, honourable people, each of whom feels bound by a duty to others, which puts them at odds. Despite appearances, deep within them they both sense that the other is deserving of trust, but they have to make a leap of faith, to listen to their heart and not the evidence before their eyes.'

Chapter One

One more door, and she would be inside his bedroom.

Jillian Marshall held her breath as she reached for the door handle, her fingers squeezing the knob gently while she turned it. She hoped to heaven the door didn't squeak when it opened.

Her eyes, adjusted to the hallway darkness, narrowed to combat the faint light under the bathroom door off to the left.

What if he's not sleeping? What if I made it past all the elaborate security precautions, only to find him wide awake? She closed her eyes for a second to steady her nerves. She hadn't spent months training to kill him for it all to come down to a call of nature destroying her plans.

Too late, she felt rather than heard someone coming up behind her—in that last moment before everything went dark.

"I'm sorry, sir. I don't know what happened," a man's shaky voice pleaded. "I never once took my eyes off the monitors, I swear it."

A deep rumble responded. "You're telling me she's invisible?"

Jillian kept her eyes closed, praying for time to decipher her situation. Her shoulders hurt from having her hands tied behind her back. The soft leather cushions beneath her helped little.

"Yes, sir—uh, I mean, no, sir." Exasperation threaded through the subordinate's tone. "I don't know what the hell happened, sir."

"Figure it out," snapped the deep voice.

"Yes, sir."

She heard the sound of footsteps scurrying toward the door. Cool air brushed over her body when it closed.

An edgy silence filled the space around her. Tension pulsated as though she lay inside a living heart. Jillian forced herself to deepen her breathing and keep it steady, her muscles relaxed. She wanted to look around her almost more than she wanted to breathe.

"You might as well open your eyes."

Not really a suggestion. His tone told her that this man was accustomed to obedience.

She lay very still, wondering which route would damn her more, to ignore him or to give in to the temptation to look.

"You're not a bad possum, but you've still got some work to do on relaxing." His words could have sounded almost amused—but for the dark slice of danger.

Jillian opened her eyes—and stifled a gasp.

Lucifer.

Black hair to his shoulders, slashed by silver at the left temple. Smoky eyes, hardening to steel as she watched. Tall…very tall, with the lean powerful frame of a warrior.

His face could have been carved from stone. High, slanted cheekbones. Dark, thick brows shadowed eyes creased by time in the sun. Strong Roman nose. A slight flexing of his jaw gave the only clue that he was less than calm. The one touch of humanity was the cleft in his chin.

She changed her mind. Maybe not Lucifer…maybe Mars, the god of war.

Who was he? Definitely not her quarry, Klaus Hafner.

Jillian stilled. This must be the man she'd heard about only in whispers. The elusive Cullinane.

"What's your name?"

"Jillian Marshall. Who are you?"

He ignored her question. "What were you doing at the door to Klaus's bedroom?" He strode around the oversize cherrywood desk to stand over her, arms crossed against his chest.

"I want a job."

One eyebrow arched.

Good. She'd surprised him.

In an instant, the mask returned. Saying nothing, he merely cocked his head, nodding slightly to indicate that he was listening.

"Was it you who stopped me?"

He shrugged his shoulders.

His control maddened her. "Your system's not so hot," she gibed. "I got through."

The momentary flash of annoyance quickly fled from his eyes. Was there nothing she could do to dent this man's armor?

She looked away, choosing to stare at the ceiling in silence, ignoring the pain in her shoulder. Pale golden light from the desk lamp threw odd shadows on the smooth creamy plaster. Rich dark paneling absorbed what little light escaped.

A very long moment passed, thick with challenge.

Drake Cullinane's scalp prickled. He could swear he'd seen a flash of emotion in her eyes at the mention of Klaus's name.

"What kind of job?"

"I want to be his bodyguard."

"Why would *you* want it?"

"I'm trained for it—and he obviously needs the help. *I* wouldn't have let anyone get through to him," she taunted.

One point to the lady. He would be chewing some butts out over this screwup. But in the final analysis, the responsibility rested with him.

As did the job of hiring bodyguards.

"I suppose you have references?" He saw her stiffen slightly, but her eyes stayed cool.

"Throw any test at me—I'll pass."

So she didn't have them. It didn't matter. No way was he hiring her, but her sheer nerve fascinated him. "Why would he want a woman as a bodyguard?"

"Because I can appear to be just a date in situations where a man would be out of place."

Intriguing concept. If he believed that was what she really wanted.

"Ah, yes, but then you can't go some places he'd have to go," he noted.

"But you always use teams anyway, so a guy can follow him into the bathroom," she retorted. "And I could be right by his side in other settings where a guy would stick out like a sore thumb."

"I like it, Cullinane," a baritone voice said from the doorway.

The woman craned her neck to follow Klaus's voice. Suddenly Cullinane regretted laying her out on his sofa like a sacrificial virgin. Hafner's voracious appetites would definitely be aroused by this woman in her black catsuit.

She was garbed in black from neck to toe, but when he'd removed her cap, a glorious fall of cinnamon hair had spilled out. For just a split second his fingers had itched to bury themselves in the rich, shiny mass. A superb foil to the black garment and the dark leather, her hair glowed like a fire breaking winter's chill.

The figure-hugging garment revealed more than it concealed. A woman in superb physical condition. Excellent muscle tone, but clearly a woman. Her breasts would fill his hands, and her hips rounded nicely from a slender waist. Cullinane swept a glance down legs that seemed to go on forever.

Oh, yes, Klaus would like it. No doubt at all.

Klaus Hafner crossed the room, navy silk dressing gown tied at the waist over only pajama bottoms. The gold chains he so adored glimmered within graying chest hair. His short, iron gray hair stood up in spikes from a restless night.

Cullinane watched Hafner's gaze roam over her body. She was a cool one, all right. Her whiskey brown eyes hardened into shards of quartz, her body utterly still as Hafner subjected her to a perusal little short of lascivious and degrading.

Hafner turned back to face him. His head jerked up in challenge. "I want her."

Cullinane stifled impatience at Hafner's impulsiveness. "You don't even know if she's competent. You know nothing about her."

"I know she came within twenty feet of me, and your system didn't catch her." Hafner's watery-blue eyes snapped with displeasure.

Cullinane gritted his teeth. "I caught her."

Hafner's eyebrows lifted. "Ah, yes, my fail-safe. My last line of defense—Cullinane." His voice drew out the long vowel in the last syllable. In chilly tones he continued. "But what if you'd slept too soundly or been—otherwise occupied? What then?"

"It's being handled, Klaus," Cullinane growled.

Hafner's smile turned expansive, though his eyes never thawed. "Oh, I have no doubt that it is, my dear friend. And I pity the man who failed in his duties." He turned back to face her, and Cullinane's gaze was drawn toward her once more. When Hafner reached out as though to touch her, Cullinane's jaw tensed, even as he wondered why in the devil he cared. After all, she'd been the one who'd barged in here.

But she was one tough cookie, this one. She wrapped an air of such icy disdain around her that

Hafner's hand hovered just an inch or two from her breast—

And then withdrew.

Hafner pivoted and crossed the room, fingers flexing. A secret smile played about his lips. When he reached the door, he stopped and spoke quietly over his shoulder.

"Check her out, Cullinane." He turned to level a stare straight at her. "I want her."

Jillian rubbed her wrists to restore circulation, feeling the deadweight of her arms turn to prickling warmth as the blood rushed back into them. Looking around the sparse room, she wondered what its normal function was. One leather-covered bench against the wall. One lamp on a nondescript table. No pictures, no drapes, no phone. Not a guest suite, that was for sure.

Beatings with a rubber hose, maybe?

Splinters under the fingernails?

She chided herself for fanciful thinking. The granite man was an enigma, true. Hardened as he was, glacial as his demeanor made him out to be, though, she couldn't see him as a sadist.

Hafner was another story.

And Cullinane was Hafner's right-hand man. That made him just as guilty.

Oh, Belinda, why didn't I pay closer attention? If I hadn't turned my back when you ran away, could I have saved you?

Shaking her head to dislodge other useless thoughts, Jillian rose from the leather-covered bench hugging the wall. She moved toward the center of the room.

Her sister was dead. Too late for the old business of regrets. Time for new business—an eye for an eye.

Hafner's insistence was the only reason she was still here, she knew. Cullinane didn't like her, didn't trust her. But thanks to Hafner's arrogance, her gamble had paid off.

Drawing a deep breath, she began the movements of tai chi, designed to bring peace and healing with its slow grace. She would need her composure to pull this off. In the belly of the beast, keeping herself focused could mean the difference between success and failure.

Between life and death.

Between obtaining a justice the system had denied and returning to her heartbroken stepmother, Loretta, empty-handed.

She had to make it right, at last, for the only mother she'd ever known. Those charged with dispensing justice to vermin like Klaus Hafner had decided to turn a blind eye.

She would not.

Loretta's despair had driven her to attempt suicide, the blood red water shocking Jillian to her marrow. Jillian had given the system chance after chance until then—but no more.

As well as she knew her own name, Jillian knew that Klaus Hafner had callously used her stepsister's body—and then murdered her because she knew too much.

The charade as his bodyguard would not be easy

to manage with hate burning a hole in her gut, but it would get her what she needed.

She would be within killing range of Klaus Hafner.

Again and again.

Cullinane might have stopped her tonight, but she'd never intended to do more than provoke interest, slipping inside their defenses. She hadn't truly believed that she could get as far as she did; thanks to someone's inattention, she'd come almost within killing range.

Except for Cullinane.

But Cullinane couldn't always be watching. She would gain their trust, prove her worth to them. Months of training added to her experience as a cop would bear fruit at some golden moment. When the time was right...

She would be waiting and watching for that moment.

Then Klaus Hafner would go straight to the hell he deserved. Arms merchant...purveyor of death...murderer.

Jillian Marshall would be the instrument of his destruction.

Now concentrate, Jillian. Clear your mind. Refresh your body. Prepare for the days to come. Get ready to show Cullinane he's wrong.

A tiny smile playing about her lips, she stretched into the next movement.

Cullinane watched her on one of the monitors in the main control room, wondering if he'd imagined the faint smile. Perhaps he had. But that was the second flicker of emotion he'd seen from her tonight.

She wasn't ice all the way down to the bottom.

Damned cool, though. Nothing she'd done so far had given him anything to explain his unease. He only sensed that something wasn't right; he couldn't put his finger on it.

But a man who'd been in deep cover as long as he had couldn't afford to ignore the slightest twinge. Tiny flickers of intuition had saved his life more than once. When you operated in a shadow world, never who you seemed to be, unable to trust anyone, you learned never to ignore your sixth sense.

Rubbing his forehead and drawing a deep breath, Cullinane fought off the fatigue that dragged at him more and more often. He'd been doing this too long. Even the most seasoned agent needed vestiges of a normal life. Friends, family, history…luxuries he couldn't afford. He had to *be* who he seemed, had to believe it to his core—yet somehow, he had to re-member that it was a charade.

Many skilled agents had fragmented under the strain.

"What do you want?" he muttered to the figure on the screen. "Why are you here?"

"Talking to yourself, Cullinane?" Hafner walked up beside him to study the same image. "Tut, tut— not a good sign in the middle of the night." He chuckled.

Cullinane spared him a quick glance and a rueful smile, then turned back to the screen.

Hafner's gaze followed his to the woman in the black catsuit. Cullinane noted every graceful move, awareness heightened by the contrast of black against the pale beige background. Her shock of red hair, falling down her back in a mass of silk, made her seem a flame, beckoning the cold, weary traveler.

"Fascinating blend of power and grace, laden with just enough sex appeal to make your blood boil," Hafner mused.

Cullinane refused to acknowledge that she had the same effect upon him. Studying her from a distance, viewing her on a small screen helped him maintain remoteness. He could admire the economy of her moves without having to feel the voltage of her presence. He could study her and figure her out.

"So she's beautiful." He shrugged. "Doesn't mean she can protect your life."

Hafner chuckled, low in his throat. "Ah, but that's what I have you for, dear boy. You'll keep me safe while I enjoy having her close."

Cullinane gritted his teeth. Hafner had become a slave to his appetites. "I haven't agreed to hire her yet."

Hafner's amusement fled. "I told you I want her, Cullinane. I'll have her, by God."

Turning to pin Hafner with his stare, Cullinane arched an eyebrow. "Even at the cost of your life?"

"You're so damn paranoid!"

"That's what you pay me to be."

Hafner's jaw flexed as he fumed.

"Don't let what's below your belt rule your good sense, Klaus. There are plenty of beautiful women around. You don't need her."

Hafner turned back to study the figure on the screen. Almost to himself, he muttered, "But she's different."

"Because she broke in to your room and could

have killed you?'' *Fool.* ''What's to say she won't do it at the first opportunity?''

''But she didn't,'' Hafner shouted.

''Because I was there in time, damn it.''

Nostrils flaring, Hafner narrowed his gaze. Almost as quickly as the anger came, it fled. Hafner began to laugh. ''Ah, but you see, that's my point. You're always there in time. I've never been safer than in your tender care.'' He leveled a look that almost spoke of pity. ''Give up, Cullinane. You know you're the best there is. Figure out some way to satisfy yourself that she can handle the job. Restrict her access to information, if that makes you feel better. Watch her closely, if that's what you need—but let me have my wish. I want her.''

''I'll try, Klaus.'' He gritted out the words. ''But for the record, I think you're a fool.''

Hafner clapped his shoulder in sympathy as he passed behind Cullinane on his way to the door. ''Yes, I'm sure you do.'' He paused, hand on the doorknob. ''But I'm the fool who has the money, now, aren't I?'' He left quietly.

Cullinane stared at the woman on the screen. He should appreciate the irony of having to convince a man whom he intended to put behind bars not to take chances with his life. He shook his head. He was not amused.

A test. He could test her skills, all right. But how could you test someone's intentions, except by giving her a chance to demonstrate them?

And then it could be too late.

Oh, he would like to see Hafner dead, himself. Like nothing better, in fact. But for now, he had to keep his eye on the prize. Dead children cried out for justice.

Cullinane wanted the whole network, Hafner and his terrorist buddies, too. He'd put years into the effort.

He'd failed once, and innocent people had died.

He wouldn't fail again. He wasn't sure he could handle another deep cover operation. Too many in a row…this would probably be his last.

He had to do it right.

Go to bed, Cullinane. You're tired. She's probably exactly what she says—just figured out a splashy way to apply for the job.

Shaking his head as he moved toward the door, Cullinane had to grin.

She'd damn sure figured out how to get their attention.

Her tai chi routine completed, Jillian ignored how much she wanted a shower and something to eat. This wouldn't be the only test she had to pass, she was sure of that.

Cullinane wouldn't just accept her word that she had the training to be a bodyguard. Even if he were less stony in his determination, he wouldn't have risen to be the right hand of such a dangerous man if he had been prone to giving trust easily.

No, it was his job to be paranoid. She just hoped she could disarm his distrust soon. Though she'd trained long and hard once she'd conceived this idea, proving herself here would be much different than excelling during training.

Relax, Jillian ordered herself. *You've got the skills.*

*You've got the motivation. You were a good cop…a
very good cop. Not many women make it on the SWAT
team. This isn't the first time you've had to keep your
head in a tense situation.*

But she had no backup this time. She was completely on her own.

She'd left the force after someone high up in government circles had quashed the investigation into Belinda's death. She was out of bounds…outside official
sanction…completely alone.

Only her *sensei*, Hiroshi, knew where she was. Her
martial arts teacher had seen through her excuses for
stepping up her training. Finally, through the lure of
sheer detachment, he'd gained her confidence.

But Hiroshi could do nothing to help her now. His
lessons were over. She would draw strength from remembering his maxim: "If one acts without fear and
with total commitment, a weaker person can defeat a
stronger one."

She'd imagined that Hafner's defenses would be
formidable, but she could never have imagined Cullinane.

Jillian settled on the floor to begin her relaxation
routine. A clear mind was essential.

*The sight of a tiny, lifeless hand holding fast to the
scrap of flannel nearly undid him.*

*Dragging one foot in front of the other, Drake
forced himself to look at it all…to see everything. The
rubble of walls that had once echoed with laughter.
The swing set twisted, mocking the life that had once
filled this place. The dust turning the grass brown,
the sunlight murky.*

His foot tripped over a mound in the dimness. Catching himself and standing upright, he looked down to watch his step.

It was then that he saw her.

An angel. Apricot curls covering her head, blue eyes staring sightlessly straight into his soul. Smooth, white cheeks utterly unmarred by the violence, pink ruffle circling her throat. White dress with tiny pink rosebuds sprinkled over the fabric. His gaze moved toward the hem and saw the torn flesh beneath.

He dropped to his knees, one hand smoothing her curls. He removed his shirt and wrapped the little girl in it, embracing her while his eyes stung and his heart burned to ashes.

Cullinane stirred from the despair that the dream always brought. He wanted to hit something. He wanted to throw up.

If he lived a hundred years, he would never forget the carnage.

If he lived a hundred years, he would never forgive himself.

Deep, rolling waves of grief rose up. Tears he could not shed burned like acid under his eyelids. His chest felt warm and sticky from the sensation of the blood he'd never been able to fully banish. Though he knew it was only a memory, he brought his hand up nonetheless. Only his bare chest, with its crisp, curling dark hair, met his hand. His shoulders sagged.

How could a merciful God let such things happen? Why were animals like the terrorists of the United Freedom Front allowed to live when innocent children died at their hands? He'd made a cold, implacable vow that the beasts who did this would pay. Years of his life had been devoted to the effort.

The dream hadn't come in quite a while. Had the woman brought it, stirring up thoughts of how much he hated Hafner?

Sitting up and lowering his legs to the floor, he bowed his head, running one hand through his hair as he tried to shake the black, bitter thoughts.

"I don't care what she wants," he growled into the air. "I'm too close to let anything stop me."

Rising heavily, Cullinane moved to dress swiftly. Drawn toward her in spite of himself, he moved toward the command post in his wing. As chief of security, he allowed no one else near his quarters, not even Hafner, without his permission. A second set of monitors banked the walls, showing every part of the compound. Only his quarters and Hafner's had no cameras planted within them.

"Who are you, Jillian Marshall?" he asked the monitor. Reaching for a switch, he almost raised the light level in the room, just to see her more clearly, to divine her intentions.

"I have a better idea," he muttered to no one at all. With swift resolution he picked up the cellular phone that switched frequencies constantly to avoid anyone monitoring their transmissions. Speaking quietly into the receiver, he issued a series of orders.

As he crossed the room, he shot one brief glance at the woman sleeping on the floor rather than the leather bench.

Tough cookie, he acknowledged with a nod. "Sweet dreams, Marshall."

* * *

The door to her prison exploded inward. Jillian jerked awake. Two figures burst into the room, and rockets of adrenaline fired through her veins. Just before the first man grabbed for her, she caught a fleeting impression. An ominous shape in the doorway, a glimpse of silver streaked across black—

Then the need to protect herself annihilated all other thoughts.

Chapter Two

The first burly form rushed at her, and Jillian's training kicked into gear. Going against instinct to block his momentum, instead she yielded, throwing him off balance. An opponent expects resistance. This man had already bunched his muscles in anticipation of her striking back. When she did the opposite, he continued to move forward, the stutter-step fouling his balance.

Jillian grasped his arm and turned, dropping below his center of gravity. Letting his momentum assist her, she pulled him over her hip and dropped him flat on his back.

She stepped away from him. The other man grabbed her from behind, wrapping an arm tightly around her body. She raised one leg and came down hard with her heel on his foot, feeling the shock reverberate through him. With a hoarse shout of pain, he dropped away, grasping for his foot as he fell.

The first man rose to his feet, brandishing a knife. His arm arced to strike. Jillian dropped down, rolling toward him in a move designed to topple his balance. He stumbled, trying not to fall, and whirled to come at her again.

A deep voice commanded, "Stop!"

Both men froze in midstep. Jillian moved quickly away from them, looking toward the sound.

Lounging negligently against the doorway, the unmistakable figure looked almost as if he'd been watching an exhibition.

A surge of anger rocketed through her, competing with the adrenaline racing through her body. Barely conscious of what she was doing, Jillian moved toward Cullinane, ready to strike.

The man with the knife jerked her back.

"Let her go, Ron," Cullinane ordered. "She won't try anything." With an almost idle challenge, he lifted one eyebrow. "Will you?"

Jillian wanted nothing worse, at that moment, than to wipe that smug look off his face.

But that would be playing his game. He wanted a reason to dismiss her from consideration. She didn't understand why, but it didn't matter. She couldn't let personalities stop her from achieving what she'd worked so hard to make possible.

Drawing a deep breath, she shook off Ron's hand. She straightened her back, issuing her own challenge with a stare. Sniffing slightly with all the hauteur she could muster, she willed the icy calm to return.

"Games, Cullinane?" She clucked her tongue,

chiding. "I'm sure it bothers you greatly that I passed your little test." Turning her back on him, she walked away nonchalantly. Over her shoulder she cast back another sally. "Surprised?"

Jillian turned to watch as the second man rose heavily from the floor, unable to put weight on his foot. Ron wrapped one of the man's arms around his own shoulders. The two started out the door.

"Is that all, boss?"

Cullinane spared them barely a glance, stepping aside to let them pass. His gaze returned to her. The smug look on his face clashed with the heat in his eyes.

So let him be mad, she decided. He didn't have to like her. Hafner wanted her; all she had to do was to prove herself competent. There would be nothing Cullinane could do.

With extreme slowness, he responded. "Yeah, Ron. Head for the infirmary. That's all—" he shot her a glance "—for tonight."

Turning his back on her, Cullinane stepped out of the room. "Sweet dreams, Marshall." He paused. "Don't assume that this door is all that's keeping you in place." Without ever looking her way again, he pulled the door behind him and left.

Not caring that someone probably watched her on a monitor somewhere, she waggled her head from side to side, her voice singsong and taunting. "Sweet dreams, Cullinane."

You coldhearted bastard.

She was good.

It stuck in his craw to admit it. Things would be

simpler if he could just say she was incompetent and leave it at that.

"Incompetent," he snorted, shaking his head. Who was he kidding? She'd breached his system, and one man's inattention was no excuse. Now she'd injured one of his best men.

Staring out the window of his bedroom, Cullinane fought the urge to go watch her again on the monitors. "This is ridiculous." He exhaled roughly. He wasn't a chauvinist; that wasn't the problem. He'd worked with other women, and damned good ones, at that. His urge to get her out of here had nothing to do with her sex.

So what was his problem? Why did she bug him so much? He hadn't let anyone get under his skin in a very long time, not even Hafner—and God knew, Hafner could drive anyone nuts.

Ruthlessly setting aside emotion, Cullinane had to admit that she'd impressed him. No small matter to put Fred in the infirmary. She obviously understood how to get around the limitations of her size.

Not that she was a small woman; he would bet she stood five-nine or so. But Fred and Ron each outweighed her by close to a hundred pounds, most likely, and both were taller.

No, his gut told him she could do the job. Smart, well trained…what other cards did Ms. Marshall have in her hand?

Shaking his head, Cullinane stripped off his clothes. He climbed into his big bed naked, as usual. Settling on his back underneath the steel gray spread, he rested his head on clasped hands. He would have to give her a shot. Only churlishness would explain not doing so.

He was a fair man; everyone knew that.

But he would be watching her every move.

"You're taking me shopping?" Whiskey brown eyes registered total astonishment. She paced the spartan room, surprisingly alert on only a few hours' sleep.

"Not my idea, I assure you," Cullinane responded dryly.

"Why?"

"You don't ask your employer why, Marshall. If you want the job, you just do it."

She looked away briefly, then back, seeming to study him closely. A brief smile curved her lips, one that vanished in an instant.

He kept his own face carefully composed, determined not to let her see how much it grated on him to have to baby-sit her. If he were honest, however, he would have to admit that he could have sent one of the other men, but he'd felt the need to observe her more closely.

"What is it that I need?"

"Hafner has a business dinner tonight at Algérie. Your catsuit won't work."

"I have my own clothes."

He shrugged. "I'm sure you do."

"Let me go get them. I'll be back in an hour."

"Where do you live?" *Who will you call while you're gone?*

"Not far."

"Good. I'll take you there later."

She glanced away. "No need. I can take care of it myself."

Ah, but I want to see your lair, tigress. "I'd rather you let me go with you."

Her eyebrows rose. "Am I a prisoner, then?" To her credit, her voice didn't waver.

"No, you're not a prisoner."

"Then I'll be back later. When do you need me?"

"You can't leave." *I won't let you.*

"Cullinane, this is just a job. I'm not an indentured servant. I can leave and come back."

"No, actually, you can't. Hafner prefers that the staff all live here."

"Hafner prefers, or Cullinane prefers to have everyone where he can watch them?"

Touché, Marshall. "Hafner prefers. Cullinane agrees."

He could almost see the gears whirring in her head. Good. Maybe she would decide that she didn't want the job so badly, after all.

After a long moment she looked back at him. "All right. But we don't need to go shopping."

"I'll know that after I look in your closet." Why did she look just the slightest bit rattled?

Because she didn't have a home but a hotel room?

"Where are you from, Marshall?"

Her glance never wavered. "Everywhere."

A hotel room. Never mind. The background check would be coming in a few days. In the meantime, he'd planned to keep a close eye on her, anyway.

"Where are *you* from, Cullinane?"

Cheeky. He'd grant her one thing; the woman hadn't bored him yet.

"Everywhere." He thought he might see tiny swirls of steam rising from her ears. But she never batted an eyelash, except for one look of reluctant appreciation.

He turned to leave. "Be ready in ten minutes."

Her sound of protest stopped him. "Cullinane, I haven't even had a shower."

Warring with himself over the temptation to allow her to take one here where he could observe, Cullinane decided that he'd better not tempt fate. Jillian Marshall had more than one weapon in her arsenal; she wasn't using that one on him.

"You can take one at your place."

An hour later, the sound of the shower running registering in the background of his thoughts, Cullinane prowled through her motel-room closet. Not the best place to stay in New Orleans, by a long shot. The advantage here was the price, obviously.

Feeling oddly like an intruder though she hadn't protested, he tried to concentrate on the garments as he slid each hanger across the rod. His mind kept coming back to the faint blush coloring her fair redhead's skin when she had let him into the room.

So the tough cookie had vulnerabilities, too.

"Get your mind on the job, Cullinane. Weakness is exactly what you want to find," he mumbled. Still, he felt a subtle sense of chagrin at her discomfort.

Even he could see the humor in worrying about that, given that he'd sicced two very tough guys on her when she was sound asleep.

Women. Too damned distracting. He understood why sailors had considered them bad luck on a voyage. It was too hard to figure out how to treat one such as Jillian, whose delicious curves beckoned but who could whip your ass if you weren't careful.

A woman should be someone you could cherish and protect. Someone you could curl up with on a cold night, whispering dreams and longings in her ear, listening to hers. Someone who'd stand beside you and build a life. When times got rough, you'd weather it together.

Someone warm. Someone tender. Not a fellow warrior.

Muttering under his breath, Cullinane snapped out of his reverie and examined her clothing. Muted and simple, these garments. Not like Hafner would want. Even Cullinane could admire the elegant lines and innate taste, though nothing here had a label to tell him who'd designed them.

If it hadn't been for his assignment with the model several years back, he wouldn't have the faintest idea, anyway. But thanks to Colette, he had a passing understanding of fashion.

"You won't find any labels, Cullinane."

He checked himself from whirling around guiltily. Too wrapped up in his thoughts, he hadn't noted the shower shutting off. He turned slowly to face her.

"Cut them off?" he forced himself to sneer. He needed distance from the sight before him.

"No. I made them."

He was mesmerized by the way the short bronze-tone kimono clung to the damp curves of her body, and it took a moment for her answer to register.

When she took the towel off her hair and bent over to rub it dry, his tongue stuck to the roof of his mouth.

The V of the robe gaped precariously. He wanted to lean closer.

Get a grip, Drake.

He loosened his tongue. "Made them? As in sewing?"

She raised her head and smiled slightly. "Want to make something of it?"

"Uh, no." He had to look away. He'd discovered just how potent her arsenal could be. "No, just surprised."

"An archaic skill for a bodyguard, right?"

He shrugged, studying the painting in front of him. His eyes strayed toward her, discovering in midstream that he had only to look at the mirror beside her to see what he wanted.

When she bent forward again, the robe slid up her thigh to reveal the smooth ivory curve of her bottom. In his concentration on that curve, he almost missed her next question.

"Will I do?"

He almost felt his neck snap as he jerked to look at her.

His eyes narrowed.

Damn it. She was doing it on purpose.

Like a cold shower, the realization brought him back to his senses. "I'll wait outside." He turned to leave.

"You didn't answer my question."

What question? Composing his face into its usual mask, he turned back. "Bring the clothes. You might as well check out when we leave."

Heading for the door, he tried to restore the balance in his favor. "They're not suitable." He didn't say that they were far too elegant for Hafner's boorish tastes. He needed to hold her at arm's length. "We still have to shop for something."

Trying to ignore the slight look of hurt that crossed her face, he left the room quickly, while he still could.

"You really want me to wear this?"

Cullinane looked up at Jillian, trying not to swallow his tongue. He'd selected several items that he knew suited Hafner's image. This was the first.

Dark green silk draped her body closely, falling to her ankles in one smooth line. The deep neckline and shoulders of the dress were encrusted with gold and green sequins, swirling over the bodice and forming a V between her breasts. The skirt was slit over one leg almost to the groin.

He shifted uncomfortably, realizing as he watched her that she really seemed ill at ease.

She looked damned good, though.

Long legs led to inevitable fantasies of them wrapped around his waist. Clearing his throat faintly, he congratulated himself on not showing what she did to him in that dress.

He hoped.

Anger at responding to her at all made him rougher than he had intended. "It's just what Hafner likes, and he's paying the bills."

Rebellion rose in her eyes. She smothered it so quickly he could almost believe he'd imagined it.

"Well, then, no need to look further."

"Go try on the others," he ordered. "You'll need more than one."

The mutinous set of her lips changed into a straight

line of resignation. She nodded curtly and left for the fitting room.

"Sir?" The saleswoman approached a couple of minutes later.

He glanced up impatiently.

"The lady asked me to tell you that she will be finished in a few moments."

He narrowed his gaze. "Tell the lady that she'd better get out here and show me each one or I'll come in there with her."

"But, sir, we can't allow—" The woman stepped away, nodding her head cautiously. "I'll tell her, sir, but I'm not sure—"

"I am," he snapped. "Tell her she has three minutes to be out here in the next one."

When three minutes had passed with no sign of Jillian, he uncrossed his legs and readied himself to rise from the chair. Even as he fumed, a part of him wanted to applaud her bravado.

But he couldn't allow it to get out of hand.

This woman could be more than a handful if he let her. She was trouble, he felt it in his bones. He'd invested years in this operation; the wheels were in motion. He would be damned if some willful redhead was going to destroy his work.

As he set his arms on the chair to rise, she flounced into the room, her eyes spitting fire, though her face stayed outwardly composed. If she held her lips any tighter, they might have to use dynamite before her next meal.

The icy mask of disdain took a little longer this time, but eventually she achieved it. Cullinane didn't try to hide his sense of victory that he'd rattled her.

For a moment, he thought about the pleasure of finding out the full range of this woman's passions. Anyone who had to clamp down that hard on emotion was bound to have very hot blood simmering beneath.

Someday, Jillian Marshall, I'm going to seek you out and stir the pot. But for right now, I'm going to make life uncomfortable enough that you'll leave.

The very red, very short dress she wore this time glistened with its solid coating of sequins; the fringe shimmied with every motion of her hips. The long, long legs made his mouth water. The deep red contrasted beautifully with her cinnamon hair, creating a stunning image. Stunning and voluptuous, yes…oh, yes.

Jillian's style…no.

"Next one," he snapped, looking away. In the mirrors he could see anger flash across her face.

She took little time before appearing in the next one, but the icy mask was firmly in place. She took as little notice of him as if he weren't even there.

Cullinane steeled himself. A slender gown of ivory silk draped her body in a column, wrapping over each breast and forming a V between curves which invited a man to look…to touch.

"Turn around," he ordered.

A tiny mutiny sprang to her lips, quickly smothered. Churlishly, she turned, but her natural fluidity would not allow her to be graceless.

He'd told her to turn before he could give himself away. The back helped little…because there was almost none of it. From the halter neck, all he could see on the way to the hollow just below her waist was skin…creamy, silky-smooth skin.

Beyond that, it didn't get much better. The gown clung to her hips like a lover before following the line of her long, elegant legs to the floor.

He raised his gaze to see her look of triumph in the mirror and knew his poker face wasn't as good as it should be.

Tit for tat, her look seemed to say.

"Next one," he snapped.

He endured a parade, knowing he punished himself as much as her in the process. He just hoped she didn't know.

Jillian's face didn't betray her distress when he purchased all but one of the gowns, but he felt it. He couldn't explain to himself why he made his next decision. He didn't explain it to her, either, just ushered her out of the store with instructions for delivery to the estate.

A few minutes later Cullinane took a seat as the discreet saleswoman at Une Belle Femme helped Jillian select clothing. The shop carried original designs and French lingerie, all with healthy price tags.

He certainly wouldn't admit, even to himself, that he wanted her to have one gown that suited her taste, much less that he might want to be the one to buy it.

This one would be payment, in advance, for what he would have to put her through in order to get her out of the way. She wouldn't know that he'd bought it himself, but he would, and it would let his conscience rest easy.

He almost groaned aloud, realizing that he felt a slight protectiveness toward her. As ruthlessly as he had lived the past ten years of his life, he tamped it down. She intrigued him too much. To be out of his way, that was all he wanted from her. Soft feelings had no place in his life.

Maybe later.

But definitely not now.

No, this was merely an apology that she would never understand, but it would salve his conscience. However much of it still existed.

After all these years in his line of work, he didn't think it would be much.

Wrapped up in his thoughts, he felt Jillian's presence register on him slowly—almost like an unconscious warming of his skin. He glanced up, surprising a soft, almost grateful expression in her eyes.

Dragging his gaze away from hers, he let himself discover Jillian's own taste. As different as night from day was her taste from Hafner's...worlds of distinction lay between.

Deep bronze silk shot with golden highlights, the gown covered virtually every inch but revealed a great deal more. Subtle elegance pervaded Jillian's choice. Long sleeves, high neck, form-fitted bodice with slender long skirt, not a slit in sight.

She turned without being asked, and Cullinane had to force himself to breathe. Only a scoop in back, revealing her delicate shoulder blades, yet it was all the more powerful for its discretion.

Powerful, hell. It was downright erotic.

Cullinane thought of the cultures he'd visited in which they understood the value of exposing only small glimpses of skin. He comprehended much better now why Victorian men could go mad over a glimpse of an ankle.

Her gown bared little…but it beckoned a man to want more.

Much, much more.

Jillian looked at him steadily in the mirror before her. He fought through the cotton his brain had come to resemble.

But she knew she had him cold.

Or hot might be the better term. He could see that she knew it.

Rising from his chair, he nodded curtly to the saleswoman to ready the bill. However much it cost, it was worth it. But damned if he'd let Jillian gloat over her effect on him.

"Get dressed, Marshall." He walked away, wondering what it would take to get rid of her.

Before he made a fatal mistake.

Chapter Three

"Cullinane." He answered the phone, his thoughts elsewhere.

"A new order for the twenty-first, Cullinane. A big one. Usual arrangements for funds transfer."

His mind snapped to immediate attention. He glanced at the calendar. Less than two weeks away. A thrill coursed through his blood. They could adjust the date for the raid to accommodate this. It was all coming together.

He answered the man he'd never seen, one of their many cutouts designed to keep anyone from knowing the whole operation and bringing it down. "References checked?"

"Clean as a whistle."

"We'll get you word of the rendezvous point."

"I'll be waiting."

A big one. Hafner had been unusually close-mouthed about this transaction. The elaborate system they'd devised meant that only Hafner and he knew the whole setup.

It had taken a long time for Cullinane to become the other man who knew everything. The habits of a lifetime were hard for Hafner to break. The swift, eager thump of Cullinane's heart came from the knowledge that Hafner wasn't telling him everything about this one.

If it was just a usual order of arms and munitions, Hafner wouldn't hedge. It looked as if the task force would get a bonus. Hafner and his old terrorist buddies must have a big one planned. The wheels were already in motion to take them all down, and now the ante would be higher. He would make sure everyone was ready.

Bile rose again in his throat as he thought of his first exposure to Hafner. Humble beginnings as a go-fer for various fringe elements had escalated into Hafner's being allowed to plant bombs, once he'd proven his worth.

It was one of those bombs that had killed the children who still haunted Cullinane's nights. New to the embassy in Rome as assistant legal attaché, he'd missed a vital clue that had allowed it to happen.

Hafner had moved up swiftly in the ranks. Shortly after that episode, he'd gotten his first line of credit. He'd bought his first consignment of arms, unloading them with panache upon some of his former terrorist colleagues at a tidy profit.

"Just a simple man of business," Hafner always said.

The business of cold-blooded murder.

Fortunately for Cullinane, colleagues in this business liked to murder one another, as well. Job advancement. Competition in the marketplace.

Whatever you called it, the higher Hafner rose, the more he needed protection from his "friends." Cullinane filled the bill nicely, with his cover as a defrocked national security agent. Klaus loved having an ex-fed on his payroll, relished knowing that someone who'd been on the other side had fallen from grace.

He compared it to having an ex-priest on your side. "Know how to say all the right words, don't you, Cullinane?" he would say, smirking. "Just can't get God to listen." He always broke into uproarious laughter at his own cleverness with that remark.

Ah, but Klaus, my dear employer, God will listen… when I decide the time is right. And then you will pay for your sins.

Cullinane rubbed his temples slowly, trying to tamp down his hopes. He hoped this was that time. He tried not to think how much he wanted out.

Jillian tried not to goggle at the ambience of Algérie. The stunning sight of crystal chandeliers showering the diners with teardrops of light, tuxedoed waiters, dressed-to-the-nines clientele…all of it fairly took her breath away.

The one-time cop living on a very modest paycheck had never experienced anything like this. She tucked her dignity around her like a cloak, held her head high and tried to concentrate on surveillance of the surroundings.

Hafner might have wanted her to wear sequins, but she wasn't ready to shoot sparkles in every direction. She hazarded a glance at Cullinane, clothed as he was all in black.

He still looked angry. He'd been madder than the devil he resembled when she'd shown up downstairs in the bronze dress, instead of one of the glitzy ones.

So why had he let her select it?

Men. Hafner had eaten her up with his eyes after Cullinane had fried her with his. If this dress wasn't to Hafner's tastes, she shuddered to think how he would behave when she wore one of the others.

The man gave her the creeps. Right now, Hafner's hand was tucked around her arm, his fingers brushing the side of her breast at every opportunity.

She had to learn to ignore it. The point of the whole exercise was to make him comfortable with her, to make him careless. She had to stop tensing at every touch, every look.

Small talk. Hafner and his business associates had talked of nothing but inconsequential matters since they'd sat down to dinner. Coffee was being served now, and so far they'd covered the Saints' season, the economic boom founded upon the casinos, plans for Mardi Gras and fishing.

Stifling her impatience, Jillian looked toward Cullinane, who'd fallen silent during the last course. She resisted a frown, seeing that his thoughts were elsewhere. *Where are you, Cullinane? So sure that nothing can happen in Algérie?*

Feeling Hafner's gaze upon her, she kept her enigmatic-smile look in place and turned to face him.

"Ah, gentlemen, I think we've bored the ladies, haven't we, my dear?"

"Why, no, Klaus, I'm utterly riveted." She batted her eyelashes for effect.

Hafner grinned. "Just as I thought. Sorry, dear heart." He stroked her neck in apology. "I think it's time we adjourned to La Mascarade for dancing." Looking around the table, eyebrows raised, he waited only a beat before rising and pulling her up with him.

Quashing the urge to pull away when he wrapped one arm around her waist and pulled her close, Jillian forced herself to relax.

"Come along, beautiful. The night is young."

Jillian put her mind into a neutral zone, refusing to feel the way he pressured her breasts against his chest briefly before releasing her to place her wrap around her shoulders. She glanced up to see Cullinane's eyes smoldering.

Why was *he* mad? She was the one getting mauled, for heaven's sake.

Turning to one of the women who had been at the table, she engaged her in conversation, lagging just behind Hafner as he strolled to the door, one arm around the shoulders of an associate. Stemming the urge to exhale in relief, she stayed close to Hafner, as she should, but was happy to be more than an arm's length away.

This was going to be more difficult than she'd imagined. Somehow she hadn't envisioned being a sexual object for him. Probably a naive omission. She'd expected to be just an employee, thought of as one of the guys. Just a bodyguard. *Not smart, Jillian.*

But it's too late. You have to deal with it until the time is right.

Deal with Mr. Itchy Fingers and with the granite man. She should have given the undercover cops she'd known more credit for what they had to endure.

When they reached the club, the sound of blues swelled up to surround her. Almost magically, tables cleared for them and drinks were ordered. Just like Algérie, it was clear that Hafner was a valued customer.

Sipping her ginger ale slowly, Jillian looked around, wishing Hafner would stop running his fingers across the bare skin at her back. She was sorry now that she hadn't picked out everything with long sleeves, a high neck and hem to the ground. Hoop skirts, that's what she would like to have right now. Or armor.

"Why don't you and Cullinane dance, dear girl?" Hafner suggested.

Jillian couldn't be sure who seemed more startled, herself or the man in black. She started to protest, though she couldn't reveal that she was a bodyguard to these people. It didn't really matter, from a safety standpoint; Cullinane had other guards scattered around them. She glanced up, hoping Cullinane would quash the idea, only to see him rounding the table toward her. No light reflected from his black garb; he looked more than a little daunting.

"Very well," she agreed. "I suppose I can do that."

Hafner chuckled. "My watchdog doesn't bite, Jillian."

She arched one eyebrow. "But has he been tested for rabies?"

The few near them who could hear over the music tittered. Cullinane's gaze burned, but his face never moved a muscle. Not your average sensitive guy.

When she hesitated, he grasped her hand in his, drawing her onto the dance floor. When they reached the center, he pulled her close to his body.

Jillian stepped back, protesting. "Shouldn't we be where we can see him?"

"My men can handle it." He pulled her back in a firm grip.

"Cullinane, I don't want to do this. Can't we just go back and say I hurt my foot?"

His jaw clenched. "It's not my choice, either, but Klaus obviously wants to talk without either of us listening. He knows the other guards can't get that close."

She wrinkled her forehead. "But why would he not want you to hear?"

"Klaus doesn't really trust anyone. His friends are only friends until they betray him, to his way of thinking."

"But you're his closest—" She stopped, confused.

"Closest what? Surely you weren't going to say 'friend'? The man has no friends, Marshall. That's how he's stayed alive this long. He merely mistrusts me less than the others. And he loves to play mind games."

"But—"

He pulled her closer, turning her body full against him. The slow, bluesy beat seeped into her bones, heating her blood along the way. "But nothing, Marshall. Be quiet and dance."

"I don't want to dance with you."

"Tough." On the crowded dance floor he swayed slowly, holding her to him with one warm hand against her exposed skin.

"Cullinane—" The slight nubby feel of his silk blazer stroked her cheek as he moved. She held herself stiffly, fighting his draw.

"Shh...it's a good song."

She tried to pull back, but his hold barred the way. His warm breath ruffled the hair at her temple. She wondered if he knew that his index finger stroked slowly between the silk and her skin.

Of course he knew. This man missed nothing.

Forced to be quiet, she felt the music work its magic, relaxing her by inches. Lulled into a strange torpor by the rhythm of the slow song, the warm, solid feel of this man, she breathed in the scent of him, an intriguing combination of sandalwood, citrus...and man.

For just a moment she forgot that he was her enemy. Male called to female as they swayed together, just on the fringes of reality. Relaxing her stance, she felt his thigh slide between hers as the sultry beat washed over them.

A slight shiver vibrated through her, and desire pooled deep within. He pulled her closer still, and she felt his body's response.

The song ended, and the crowd around them moved away. For one breathless second their gazes met, the smoke from his gray eyes curling deep inside her. Then gray hardened to steel as if he'd shaken off a dream. Jillian felt him tense and she jerked back, anger surging as she remembered who he was, what he represented. Loathing filled her that for even one moment she could forget why she was here.

Presenting her back to him, she headed off the dance floor. He didn't follow. When she glanced back over her shoulder, she saw him standing very still, his mask firmly in place.

It never happened, she told herself. Catching Hafner's curious look, she squared her shoulders. There lay her goal. Nothing, and no one, would stop her. Not even Cullinane. Not even though he made her mouth go dry. He wasn't made of only stone, though—she knew that now. Well...maybe part of him. She repressed a grin.

That thought cheered her. *Hope you hurt, Cullinane. Hope you suffer. Maybe you'll slip up and give me the chance to hurt Hafner.*

Now, there was a thought. Could she play Cullinane well enough to compromise him?

Jillian shook her head. Not in this lifetime. Hafner was enough of a handful. The granite man ate girls like her for breakfast. Better not play that game.

The sobering thought steeled her and helped her make it through the rest of the evening, through Hafner's pawing—and Cullinane's stony stare.

At five-thirty, as always, Cullinane began his workout, pushing himself harder than usual to punish himself for last night's lapse.

Was he out of his mind? It had been years since he'd been led around by his— Swearing darkly, Cullinane focused on the weights he pressed. If he wasn't careful, he'd get injured. That was the last thing he needed, if his opportunity was really at hand.

His gut told him it was.

Even though he hadn't been able to listen to Hafner's conversation once they reached the club, he still knew. Something about Hafner's suppressed excitement conveyed the message. His eyes had gleamed from more than the hots he had for Jillian.

Marshall, damn it. Don't think about her as a woman. He wouldn't think about her silky skin…her curves, which fit so perfectly against him…the cradle between her thighs that he—

Cullinane cursed vividly. If he was going to be an idiot and lift this much weight without a spotter, the least he could do was not get distracted. He'd gone too long between women, that was all. He had little taste anymore for meaningless encounters, and a relationship was out of the question for a shadow man. He had women he could call, women for whom casual was perfect. He'd better take the edge off before he did something stupid.

Gritting his teeth, he concentrated on his technique. Sweat broke out on his forehead when he added one more lift to his second set as a reminder. Two hundred twenty-five pounds had never felt heavier.

You're not twenty-five anymore, Drake. This close to forty, you'd better be more careful with your body. He put everything he had into one more lift, muscles screaming for release.

You can do it. You can do it. Go for it.

Exultation swelled within him as he rested the bar safely on the rack above him. Never mind that his arms felt like jelly now. Suffering strengthened the mind.

Right.

Suddenly, though he hadn't heard the door open, he knew he wasn't alone in the gym. It was at the far end from the bedroom wings, and he usually had it to himself at this early hour. Swearing under his breath, he wondered who dared disturb him in his present mood.

He should have known.

Looking into the mirrored wall beside him, he saw the indecision on her face harden into resolve. Turning her back on him, Jillian began to stretch.

He stifled a groan. Couldn't a man even work out in peace?

Cullinane rose from the bench and moved over to the stair stepper. Climbing two hundred flights of stairs in twenty minutes would cure him of watching her behind when she bent over to stretch.

Hell.

Cullinane closed his eyes and started climbing.

Jillian wished there weren't so many mirrors in this place. Everywhere she turned, she could see his reflection. Every muscle outlined, every drop of sweat that plastered his tank top against that broad chest, the way his knit gym shorts molded and cupped—

Stop it, Jillian. Get to work. She gritted her teeth at the knowledge that this might be the only free time she could claim in a day. She hoped with her last breath that this was a unique event—that Cullinane didn't usually work out at this time of day. Could she afford to let her conditioning slide just to avoid being near him?

He was just a guy, for Pete's sake. She'd worked out with guys for years.

None of them had made her throat close up, though. No matter how good he'd looked in his clothes, seeing him sweaty and nearly naked made it all too real how he would look in the act of—

She sighed and resolved to add twenty crunches for punishment. No more wayward thoughts. Good grief, the man could barely stand to have her around.

He was different last night, Jillian.

She couldn't explain it, though. This was the same man who'd sicced two big toughs on her when she was sound asleep. Last night had to be an anomaly.

Had to be. He protected her enemy—that was all she needed to know.

Last night was just hormones. Hormones could be ignored.

Jillian squeezed her eyes closed and added ten more crunches.

"Spot me?"

The husky voice startled Cullinane, so intent was he upon climbing the last two flights of stairs.

"What?" He glanced over his shoulder, feeling her gaze move over him.

"Pretty impressive, Cullinane. Not just a lazy supervisor, are you? You've been climbing for twenty minutes. How many flights is that?"

He held up one finger for her to wait, needing his breath to finish off smoothly.

"Sorry."

He stepped down, reaching for his towel, unable to avoid a sense of pride that his breathing wasn't labored. "Two hundred."

She whistled in appreciation. For a moment they shared a grin.

"How about a spot?" She walked toward the bench press, casting a gibe over her shoulder. "Not all of us are so foolhardy as to lift that kind of weight with no spotter."

Cullinane felt an unaccustomed flush. "I know what I'm doing."

Her glance swept his body. "Oh, I don't doubt that for a minute." She began adjusting weights on the bar, handing the excess weights to him. "But it's still a bad idea."

He stifled a sharp retort. She was right. It was a bad idea. Normally more cautious, he'd had some frustrations to burn off this morning.

Most of them caused by the woman standing next to him.

"So how much do you want to lift?" He indicated the bar with a nod of his head.

"A hundred."

He issued his own whistle. "Pretty impressive…"

Jillian shot a glance his way. "For a girl, you mean?"

Give credit where credit is due. "For anyone who weighs close to a hundred pounds less than I do."

She seemed appeased. "How do you know what I weigh?" A secret smile played about her lips.

He moved toward the racks holding the weights. "I don't." He shot her what he hoped was an impersonal glance, shrugging. "Seems safe to guess that it's a lot less than any of the other bodyguards.'' He hoped his voice was steadier than his pulse.

Her gaze studied his in the mirror for a long moment, then she drew away, settling down on the bench.

He released a breath, moving to stand behind her head, his gaze drifting across her supple body, taking in the sight of her black halter top...the bare creamy skin at her taut midriff...the skin-tight black shorts hugging well-defined thighs—

Dangerous thoughts, Drake. He cleared his throat. ''Ready?''

Her gaze caught his for one suspended moment. He couldn't decipher her expression. ''Yeah,'' she replied, reaching up for the bar.

He lifted it off the rack and handed it to her, oddly reluctant to burden her with it. Still, he pulled his support away smoothly.

An odd feeling, this, watching someone whose graceful body he'd held in his arms last night use that same body with such power and strength now. No question that she knew what she was doing. No neophyte would be pressing this much weight for her size.

Impressive, he had to admit. Her body was a finely honed machine, exhibiting great strength and the legacy of obvious discipline.

Yet she was all woman, no question. Jillian's muscular definition was imposing when she exerted herself, like right now, yet when she simply moved about in the normal course of things, she looked undeniably feminine—no bulging biceps or mannish features.

''Stop smirking.''

Glancing down, he could see that she really had her dander up. "I wasn't smirking." He smiled. "Don't talk. You could get hurt."

She glared at him, then focused on the middle distance, concentrating as if he weren't there.

Peeved, maybe. Definitely not mannish. Cullinane smiled again.

"Twelve." She pushed the bar toward the rack.

He took it out of her hands and settled it carefully. Jillian sat up, pausing as if to consider her next words. Looking sideways at him, she asked, "Then what were you thinking, if you weren't smirking?"

That damned smile held an allure he didn't need to notice. *Turn away, Drake, before you get into deep water.*

"Nothing to do with you. Something much more important."

The swift hurt that crossed her face shouldn't have bothered him.

Cullinane headed toward the door to the outside, then hesitated. "You finished? Any more sets?"

She had her you-can't-bother-me look back firmly in place. "No." She turned away.

Feeling as if the hot breath of disaster hovered over him, Cullinane left for his run, one step ahead of the urge to turn back.

Jillian peered down the road as she ran, looking for a good place to turn around. She'd finished her indoor workout and had decided a run would do her good. Cullinane had left the gym abruptly; she had no idea where he'd gone.

Stop thinking about Cullinane. Think about Hafner. Think about what you learned last night.

Hafner was a creep. No news there. He was much worse than a creep; he'd murdered her sister.

A hot ache seized her chest at the thought of the last, angry words she and Belinda had exchanged.

"Stop telling me what to do with my life, Jillian," Belinda had all but screamed. "I'm not your little sister anymore. You were never my real sister. You're only a stepsister, and I'm sick of you looking down your nose at my choices." Belinda's blue eyes had snapped with the emotion spilling over her lashes. "He loves me, and you're just jealous!"

Just jealous...just jealous...never my real sister...sick of you looking down your nose... Could there have been any truth to Belinda's accusation?

A horn blasted Jillian out of her thoughts, the squeal of tires accompanying the blaring noise. She jumped off to the shoulder, her breath coming in quick gasps.

"What the hell are you doing?"

She whipped around to see Cullinane headed toward her from a side path. He must have been running nearby.

"Lady, are you crazy or what?" The driver of the car that had nearly hit her leapt out, his expression thunderous. "Do you know how close I came to hitting you?"

Her head swerved from side to side as she backed away, trying to placate both of them while stilling her rapid-fire pulse.

"I'll take care of it. Are you all right?" Cullinane

spoke to the driver, his voice sounding faint in her ears.

"Yeah, I'm all right, but your girlfriend here better watch where she's going. She could be dead right now."

She heard Cullinane's deep voice murmuring to the man as he escorted him back to his car. "No harm done," he called out, and the man pulled away.

Oh, man. Here it came. A great excuse for him to read her the riot act.

He stopped in front of her, saying nothing. Her attention caught on one drop of sweat rolling from his throat down tanned skin, disappearing into the dark hair above the neck of his tank top. She wondered idly how long it would take to join the moisture soaking through the fabric over his chest.

When he remained silent, she raised her eyes to his.

The usual steely gaze studied her. His jaw flexed. "Are you all right?" An odd huskiness tinged his voice.

She hesitated, caught by his tone, then nodded her head. "Yeah. I was…preoccupied. I'm sorry."

She could almost see the thoughts whirring in his head as he started to speak, then stopped abruptly. Nodding his head, he glanced down the road, back in the direction she'd come. "Let's head back."

Then he turned away and with strong, steady strides headed toward the compound. Jillian watched him, still surprised that she'd escaped a lecture. Cullinane glanced back, one imperious eyebrow lifted, and she straightened, determined not to show him weakness.

He slowed his steps enough for her to catch up, then stride for stride they matched their styles to one another. Jillian felt an odd sort of kinship she'd never expected to feel with him.

The sight of the compound abruptly reminded her that this man was her enemy. His success would mean her failure. The thought that she could respond at all to a man who would protect a vicious beast like Hafner shook her deeply. Drawing upon her last reserves of energy, she sprinted ahead of him, covering the final yards to the gate, reminding herself that she could afford no distractions.

She had responsibilities. She had a mission.

She could not fail.

Chapter Four

Sunday after lunch, Drake drove toward Metairie on autopilot, restless and uneasy. Good thing that his regular contact with his handler from the Bureau was today; he had too much on his mind, and arranging for special meets was rough, as tightly controlled as he'd made Hafner's compound.

A wry smile quirked his lips. Hafner thought Drake was meeting a hooker on these outings; Frank Campbell might resent being thought of that way. It was a good cover, though—Hafner took delight in chiding him for not bringing women to the compound, offering to provide him with all the free company he could ever want.

Drake rubbed the bridge of his nose. Soon. It would all be over soon. Then he could start washing away the years of filth staining his soul from close contact with vermin like Hafner.

Pulling around the motel, he parked the car and headed for the ground-floor room that a stunning blonde would have checked in to a half hour ago. Lisa Porter, a rookie agent, would soon be watching television in one room while he met with Campbell in the connecting room.

The door to the room swung open before he could knock. Slender arms wrapped around his neck for the benefit of anyone tailing him, one long, black-stockinged leg rubbing against his as ruby red lips met his own.

When he realized that he was comparing the feel of her to Jillian, he cursed silently and took the blonde's kiss deeper. When he set her back from him, her breathing was unsteady, her eyes wide with shock.

"Well, glad to see you, too, big guy."

"Okay, Agent Porter, that's enough." Frank Campbell stood up from the table in the connecting room's shadowed corner. "I think your show's on." The medium-height, fiftyish agent shook Drake's hand, then ushered him into the room and shut the connecting door. John Alonzo, the case officer, nodded to Drake.

Lisa would be watching the parking lot, using the sound of the television to muffle any missing sounds of passion from prying ears. The noise served a purpose, but Drake had always wondered at people who made love with the television blaring. He knew it happened, but somehow he thought they couldn't be paying enough attention to the nuances of pleasure. A romantic, perhaps, but he'd always thought his partners, however casual, deserved his full and complete attention.

"You okay, Morgan?" Alonzo's use of his real name jolted Drake.

Damn. That was the problem. Jillian Marshall was a distraction he didn't need. He'd never thought about passion at one of these meets before.

He nodded. "Yeah. Just thinking." He sat down, repressing a surge of excitement. "I think we might get a bonus."

Alonzo's head jerked up from his notes, his dark eyes narrowing. "What's happening?"

"A big shipment coming in on the twenty-first. Hafner's playing it very close to the vest with me, lots of phone calls on his unmonitored line. Usually he likes to puff about the size of his haul. He seems nervous, but excited. My gut tells me it's big. A nice bonus to add to the haul on this raid."

"I'll alert the team to make adjustments. We'll be in touch. Still think he'll run it through the bayous?"

Drake nodded. "Something this important to him, it only makes sense. It's too hard to track shipments being threaded up through bayou country." Going through major ports meant involving too many people and risking detection. Hafner had always used smaller craft to send and receive his shipments in bits and pieces. More time-consuming, to be sure, but much safer from detection. Less loss if the loot is divided and something goes wrong.

He was also economical; the same craft that moved arms one way generally shipped cocaine in the other. No sense wasting transportation. "Just business sense," Hafner would say.

"So tell me about the progress on your end," Drake prompted.

Alonzo leaned forward. "We go to the grand jury tomorrow to get the indictments in place. We'll adjust the arrest date to the twenty-first and coordinate with the Germans and Italians." He smiled. "We're in good shape, Morgan. It's going to work."

"We'll move to Delta phone contact system, effective immediately." Frank rummaged through his notebook. "Here are the numbers we'll have staffed around the clock. This one's your primary get-out number if anything goes wrong. And we've got yours already."

Drake scanned the printout, drawing out his palmtop computer and quickly entering the numbers into files under various women's names. Should anyone break his password, it would look like the names of his "hookers." If someone persisted enough to call, each of these would be answered with varying escort service names.

He didn't kid himself that Hafner couldn't have someone watching him as closely as he watched everyone else for Hafner. He'd made his quarters safe, but that was his only refuge. Even there, he still took precautions.

Closing the cover on his palmtop and settling back, Drake waited for Frank to stop writing notes to himself.

Without raising his head, Frank spoke up. "So what's got you so edgy?"

"This operation isn't enough?"

Frank stared. "You don't rattle easy."

Drake sighed. He wasn't ready to discuss Jillian—with anyone. He had no choice, though. "There's someone new around—a woman."

Frank's gaze held steady. "Hafner's new one?"

Drake shook his head.

"Why's she there?"

"Says she wants to be a bodyguard." He chuckled, remembering. "She picked a hell of a job application." Proceeding to tell them where he'd finally stopped her that first night, he could appreciate his handler's lifted brows.

"We could use her on our side." Frank paused, head cocked to one side. "So what are you going to do about her?"

I wish I knew. Shaking his head, Drake glanced away, studying the print of sailboats on the wall. "Something's not right, but I don't know what." He straightened in his chair. "All I know is that I don't like the distraction. She's good, but I'm going to make her life difficult. I don't want her around, not now, but Hafner's determined."

"Think Hafner's got her there to watch you?"

He gave it some thought, then shook his head. "I don't think so. Hafner wants her, but not so she'll spend time with me."

"That good-looking, huh?"

Ruefully, he nodded. "Yeah."

"Going to distract you?"

"No way." Drake met Frank's gaze evenly. "I've waited too long for this."

"Want me to run a check on her?"

"Yeah, probably, but let's see what my routine check pulls up first. I'll let you know." He rose, not wanting to discuss Jillian further.

"You hang in there, Drake. Maybe it's almost over."

He wondered if he'd ever be free of Hafner. Ever get to live like other people. "You ever take your kids to an amusement park, Frank?"

The hazel eyes widened, then softened in sympathy. "Yeah, sometimes." He rose, too, crossing the room and clapping Drake on the shoulder. "You wanna go next time?"

Drake chuckled. "No, thanks. I might go fishing, though, when this is over."

"I'll buy the worms."

Smiling, Drake turned toward the door. "I'll be in touch."

"I hope this is it." With a short nod, Frank turned back to the table.

Not half as much as I do. Outside, Drake sat in the car for a minute, feeling the split in his mind and trying to bridge it, readying himself to head back to the world of the man known only as Cullinane.

Jillian looked out her window at the lush grounds below, her eyes focused on nothing but the despair that dogged her.

She couldn't do this. Couldn't pull it off. Despite all her planning and preparation, she was going to fail. Her plan was good—it wasn't that which disturbed her so. It was that she'd never factored in how hard it would be to be this alone, to hold all the strangeness at bay with no respite.

She'd come into this like John Wayne or someone, thinking that she'd find it easy to hold herself apart. But she hadn't counted on Cullinane. Hafner gave her the creeps, but Cullinane scared her to death. He was real, and he was serious. He could ruin it all.

*Why don't you just say what you mean, Jillian?
Something about him draws you, and you're wondering what that says about who you really are.*

Pushing away from the window with both hands, then diving her fingers into her hair, she paced the floor. She was afraid to go out there, but she couldn't stay in here forever. She'd never find the weaknesses of this place if she didn't probe.

She'd never envisioned it going so slowly. Right now she wanted nothing more than to be in and out of here, quick and clean.

But it wouldn't be that easy. Luck had played a part in how far she'd made it that first night. But Cullinane wasn't a man who made mistakes. Too controlled and precise, too quietly dangerous.

She almost thought he was more dangerous than Hafner.

But he wasn't vicious. Somehow she didn't think he was evil, either—but she couldn't be sure.

Why was he here? Was he so morally bankrupt that Hafner didn't bother him?

She had to get out of this room, out of her thoughts. Swift fingers braided her still-damp hair, then she slipped on her sandals, sparing no glance at the mirror. Headed for the door, she stopped suddenly.

Hafner. She was the spider, he would be the fly. *Better go put on some lipstick, Jillian. Try some earrings.*

Jillian shuddered, then squared her shoulders and headed for her private bath. When she'd fastened slender gold dangles to her earlobes and dabbed mocha cream on her lips, she checked to see that the deep green of her tank top worked with the khaki of her shorts. Grabbing a book from her nightstand, she headed out to scout the grounds, a good reading place her ostensible destination. As she turned the door-knob, she drew in a deep breath.

Patience, Jillian. And watch your back.

Strolling the grounds a few minutes later, she glanced back up to check the location of her room. On one balcony stood Klaus Hafner, his gaze hot on her. She turned away and kept walking.

Showtime.

A small glade she'd passed on her way into this compound was nearby. Entering the clearing, she saw a small gazebo nestled beneath the trees, lacy ferns hanging at intervals under the eaves. Off to her right, she saw the clear turquoise of pool water, cool and inviting. She walked up the two steps to the gazebo and settled on flowered cushions, hearing the lazy whir of the ceiling fan overhead—perfect for the cooler October temperatures. Opening her book, she settled in to wait, soon deep in the story.

"A beautiful bodyguard who reads romance novels. You are, indeed, an unusual woman."

Hafner's voice startled her. Marking her place slowly, she raised her gaze to his.

He crossed the gazebo toward her, eyes challenging. Just when he got so close her heart all but seized in her chest, he veered away, coming to stand near her head, just past her vision.

His voice came from above her. "What do you think of my little kingdom?"

Jillian felt his body heat; he stood only inches away from her right shoulder. She stared out at a very old magnolia, refusing to scoot away. "It has...a certain grace.'' Turning her gaze up in his direction, she continued, ''Did you do it?''

His gaze arrowed into hers, chilling and direct. For one terrifying second, it was as though she'd seen into the mind of a madman, as though both their minds had zeroed in on the same point in space. Her words reverberating in her mind, she realized that her question had two layers—she could be asking him if he'd killed her sister just as easily as inquiring about the decorating.

The moment spun out until her nerves sang with tension. Chilled to the bone, she sensed the breath of evil within him.

Then he swung his gaze away from her, and she felt as if a spell had been released. Closing her eyes briefly and struggling for calm, she barely heard his words.

''Some things I have others do…but some things I prefer to do myself.''

He couldn't know. She was here under another name. She and Belinda looked nothing alike. Lifting a hand, she massaged at the painful thump of her heart.

Calm down, Jillian. You're spooking yourself. He doesn't know who you are.

When his finger skimmed her nape, she shivered, rising to her feet and moving away.

''Running away, Jillian Marshall?''

Lifting her chin, she forced herself to turn around, only to discover him right in front of her. She stood her ground. ''No. Just tired of sitting.''

His gaze was amused. She'd never felt more like prey being toyed with by a predator.

You could kill him right now, Jillian. You could disable him and then kill him. You know how.

A metallic flash behind him caught her gaze. One of Cullinane's men, patrolling the grounds.

No. She wasn't on a suicide mission. She would bide her time.

Carefully shielding her thoughts from him, she kept her gaze lowered, the gold chains in his salt-and-pepper chest hair catching her eye. The contrast with Cullinane's muscled, golden chest couldn't have been more pronounced.

Hafner placed a finger under her chin, drawing it upward. Knowing what was coming, she kept her eyes closed. She'd never make it if she had to look at him. Feeling his evil was more than enough. She sensed his head drawing nearer and steeled herself for the touch of his lips.

"I don't think that's part of the job description, Marshall."

Cullinane. Waves of relief swept through her. She whirled toward the source of his voice.

Hafner swore darkly. "It's Sunday, Cullinane. It's her day off."

"She doesn't get a day off, Klaus. She hasn't passed muster yet. We've got testing to do before I sign on to keeping her around. Today's as good a day as any." The steel in his gaze dared either of them to argue.

"I'll send her along in a few minutes."

"Not if you want me to stay on the job."

Jillian froze, astonished that Cullinane would up the ante so high. Torn between anger and relief, she crossed her arms over her chest. "What kind of testing?"

He ignored her, his gaze still challenging Hafner's.

When Hafner looked away, then stepped back, she fought not to exhale loudly in relief. But it was only a temporary respite—making herself into bait might very well be the only way to get Hafner away from the others.

Then Hafner chuckled, stepping down from the gazebo. "Got a piece today, didn't you, Cullinane? Why isn't your disposition better?"

"My disposition will improve once she proves herself—or she's gone."

"I've already spent good money on gowns for her. I expect you to find her sufficient—or finish her training yourself." Good humor restored by reasserting his power, Hafner turned and cast her a heated glance. "We must resume our discussion later, I'm afraid. My watchdog wants to beat his chest."

Jillian didn't look at him, noting the brief flicker of anger across Cullinane's face.

Hafner walked away, hands in the pockets of his shorts, whistling.

Cullinane's jaw flexed, his eyes hard as granite. "Come on," he snapped. "Unless you'd rather give up and leave now."

Jillian's chin jutted forward. "Not on your life, watchdog." She brushed past him, hands clenched in fists.

"Marshall." His quiet tone stopped her.

She didn't turn.

"Don't be alone with him, if you don't want to play."

She swallowed hard. "I think that's my business, don't you?"

After a long pause, he stepped up beside her, his size imposing. She refused to turn around, just stared straight ahead.

"Everything here is my business." His warm breath blew across her forehead. After much too long a moment, he stepped around her. "This way, Marshall."

She followed him without a word.

"This place is amazing," Jillian commented as they entered a wing of the compound he hadn't yet shown her. Cullinane saw her glance across the hallway to a room filled with mats, where two of his men were matched against one another in practice combat.

Cullinane saw Fred look up from where he stood watching, his gaze on her angry but wary. The cast on his foot would be there for weeks; until it came off, he was stuck with paperwork and video surveillance. He wouldn't forgive Jillian easily for the ribbing he'd taken from the other men.

Fred saw him and flushed, turning back to watch the combatants.

Cullinane held the door open for her, noting her surprise at the courtesy. Good. Keep her off balance.

Jillian entered the darkened alcove outside the firing range, heading toward the opening.

"Marshall." When she turned, he held out a set of hearing protectors, complete with earplugs.

She approached him warily, not meeting his gaze as she opened the small pouch and began inserting the earplugs with quick competence, settling the headset around her neck. Walking around him, she plucked a set of goggles from the board behind him, then settled her hands on her hips.

"Do you still have my weapon?" she demanded.

He nodded, remembering how she'd balked at going out the other night without one. Walking over to a locked cabinet, he pulled a key ring from his pocket and opened the doors. Plucking her Walther PPK from its slot, he turned and handed it to her, retaining his own grasp on it.

Irritation flared in her gaze, quickly masked. Whiskey eyes rose to meet his, her look cool and indifferent.

Holding on for another moment, he slowly released her weapon. She stepped back, checking it over, her movements quick and clean. No question she'd done this many times.

Cullinane didn't reach for his own SIG-Sauer at the small of his back. He might practice later, but he was here to test her. Gesturing to the doorway, he urged her to precede him.

Watching the long braid swish across her back, seeing her pale skin above the deep green top, he understood completely why Klaus would want her.

But how much did she want Klaus? He hadn't missed the quick flare of relief in her eyes when he'd interrupted them. Little fool. She was playing with fire. Klaus was vicious. He would use her and discard her like used tissues.

Did she want his money? To get in on his deals? What? What brought her here? Surely it was more than just job advancement. No question that she could name her price after working here, if she did her job right. And she'd been smart in her thinking—women in this field were still uncommon but they could play crucial roles men couldn't.

He didn't know the answers. But he would break her down and find out. She was a cool customer, but there was fire beneath that ice. He'd keep probing for weakness until he figured her out.

And hope, in the meantime, that she didn't screw everything else up. She was dangerous and unpredictable.

Cullinane didn't like either one.

Stepping up behind her at her platform, he decided to start rattling her cage right now.

"You're crowding me." She spoke over her shoulder.

"Just watching." He saw her frame tense as she sighted.

"How do you know I won't jerk back with the kick?"

"Good try, Marshall."

She turned halfway toward him, her shoulder against his chest. He hadn't given her room to step away.

Her gaze rose, eyes narrowing. "Trying to rattle me, huh?"

He glanced down, thinking he'd be smart to step back himself. Teeth clenched, he felt his body stir at the feel of her. "Is it working?"

"No." With a dismissive toss of her head, she turned back to face the target. Delicate gold earrings dangled with her movement.

It didn't matter. He'd seen her gaze waver.

As if to taunt him, she leaned back slightly and

rubbed her bottom across the front of his jeans in one quick stroke.

Hot, dark need seared down his spine. It took all his control not to groan.

To get even, he slowly brought his hands up her sides, barely brushing fingers along the outside curves of her breasts before sliding them down her arms and closing his hands over hers. Her slender back burned his chest where they touched.

"Try it this way."

She hissed, then gritted out, "Very funny, Cullinane."

He wasn't smiling. "Are we having fun yet?"

Jillian broke away, jerking the headgear down around her neck. She turned to face him. "Fun? Do you know the meaning of the word?"

He frowned. "What do you mean?"

Golden lights sparked in those brown eyes as she challenged, "Do you ever smile? Fool around? Do anything at all lighthearted?"

Stung, he responded, "Of course I do." *I think.*

"I don't think so. You're too busy intimidating the hell out of everyone around you. It's part of your image—the dark warrior Cullinane knows all, sees all, hears all, and don't ever cross him."

"Does it work?"

She turned away, not answering.

He turned her back to him, gripping her shoulders. Touching her was a mistake—it made her too real, too tempting. "We're not here to have fun, Marshall. If that's what you want, then you'd better pack now."

Jillian set her weapon down. "You'd like that, wouldn't you?" Arms crossed over her chest, she was the picture of defiance, steam all but rising from her ears.

He smiled. Redheads and temper. The old adage must be true.

"Go to hell, Cullinane. I've met guys like you before. I've had to prove myself every time." She sniffed, turning away. "I'll show you, too." Resettling the headgear, she picked up her weapon again and took aim. "Now back off."

She fired, her shot clean and true. Turning toward him, she smirked, then turned back, squeezing off several rounds.

Calling for a new target, she loaded a new magazine, studiously ignoring him.

After firing off the other rounds, she stepped away, lowering the headgear to her neck.

"Okay, hotshot. What's next?"

Damn her. Eyes bright with temper, chest heaving with repressed emotion, she stirred him more than ever. He would like to take her to the ground here and now, spark that temper into passion, surround himself with the life that brimmed from her and warm his cold, dark soul.

Instead, he would have to keep trying to break her, to take that wild spirit and crush it, to make this strong, gutsy woman doubt herself so she would leave, tail tucked between her legs.

Of all the hard things he'd ever done in his work, this might be the most obscene.

Chapter Five

"Across the hall," Cullinane ordered. His gaze held an odd light of something Jillian would almost call—regret? He turned away too quickly for her to check again, but she shook her head. No, couldn't be. He was enjoying every minute of this. And she'd helped him by losing her temper.

Her temper had always been a problem. She shouldn't have given him the satisfaction of seeing her angry. Cold and rational, just like him, that's what she had to be.

But remembering the feel of him surrounding her, warmth singeing her back, Jillian knew cold was asking a lot of herself.

Then she recalled the one feel she'd had as she brushed him. And smiled.

He wasn't immune to her, either.

Two can play this game, Cullinane.

Pulling off her hearing protectors and goggles, removing the plugs from her ears, she picked up her weapon and followed him to the other room. Handing the protective gear to him, she retained her weapon.

He stood at the guncase, waiting, doors open, watching her.

For a long moment she stared at him, pondering the price of insisting on keeping her weapon. Finally she turned it butt out and placed it in his palm. Something like understanding flared in his gaze.

"No weapons allowed in the practice room," he explained. "Tempers get hot sometimes." He placed his own weapon inside, closing the door and locking it. "I'll give it back to you once we're done."

He did understand how naked she felt without it. Maybe he was human, after all.

The next few moments gave her doubts. As they entered the practice room, every eye in the place was on her, and none of them friendly. The blond man she'd bested the night she came stood against one wall, walking cast on his foot and deep, burning anger in his gaze. If he could have been the one to take her on, she was certain he would have jumped at the chance.

"Take your pick, Marshall," Cullinane offered.

Jillian scanned the handful of men in the room. Every one of them looked more than happy to be chosen, as though avenging their comrade were top choice on the menu. The second man who'd been in the room that night stood across from her, hands on his hips, gaze all but daring her to choose him.

She stifled a sigh. She'd had to prove herself over

and over, first when she'd dared try out for the boys' baseball team in high school, then at the academy. She straightened, understanding how the game was played. You wanted respect, you took on the big dog.

"I choose you, Cullinane."

He looked startled, then frowned.

"What's the matter, hotshot? Afraid I'll embarrass you in front of your men?"

A look of reluctant amusement lit his gaze, as if he understood her game. Still, he had to know that once the challenge was thrown out, he had no choice.

"In case you hadn't noticed, Marshall, I'm a lot bigger than you."

She saw the smirks on the faces around the room, everyone no doubt hoping she'd blink. "So?" She waved a hand. "Everyone in here's bigger than me." Upping the ante, she threw out, "I've done it before." Shooting a glance across at the man with the cast, she taunted, "They didn't like it when I won, either."

Cullinane almost smiled at that, but she didn't like the fierce gleam in his eye. He began removing his shoes. "You're on, hotshot." He threw her jeer back in her face. "But don't expect me to take it easy on you." He nodded toward a closed door, then tied his hair back. "Pads are in there, if you want them."

Hoping she didn't regret this decision, she shook her head. "I won't have them on when the bad guys come." And she had to prove she could take it.

Cullinane shrugged. "Suit yourself."

She removed her sandals, heading off the mat to set them out of the way. Expectation lifted the mood of the room. She could all but hear their lips smacking at the prospect of her defeat.

It couldn't happen. She couldn't let it. Too much needed to be proven to these men, but more important, to Cullinane—and herself. She'd won against bigger men before. Bigger wasn't always better, especially very muscular men who often didn't have her agility.

And she wasn't a lightweight herself. She took a deep breath to calm her nerves and get centered, hearing Hiroshi's voice in her head.

Use his cockiness against him. Watch for the advantage, and let him defeat himself. Drawing another deep breath and searching for the mind's center as she'd been taught, she prepared herself to win.

When Jillian turned and moved toward him, Cullinane could see the light of battle in her eyes. Her body straight and tall, resolve spoke from every line of her frame.

Damn, she was a hellcat. He'd never met a woman like her in his life. A moment's regret flared that they'd met in these circumstances, then she softened her body into limber waiting, arms out to defend, and he readied himself for her first move.

Reluctant admiration struck when he realized she was going to make him move first. Clever—she knew it was a mistake to be the first to commit, but he'd bet anything that she sensed how impatient their audience was and was betting that he'd move first to satisfy the blood lust of the others.

But she was wrong. He'd proven himself long ago. His men could wait there until hell froze over, for all he cared.

Suddenly she was inside his guard, moving to

strike. He reacted quickly, turning her and flipping her onto her back.

But quick as a cat she was back on her feet, eyes sparking, cheeks bright with anger. A snort of laughter from Fred didn't help. To her credit, though, she didn't lose her composure. She circled him slowly, looking for weakness, head held high and proud.

He moved in on her, only to have her foot meet his chest hard enough he knew he'd bruise. Before he could unbalance her, however, she'd danced away, eyes alight with challenge.

Arms in motion, he closed in sideways. Quickly she turned, sliding under his arm, delivering a quick blow to the liver. Stung, he whirled, grasping her arm and pulling her to him with one quick jerk, arm sliding across her chest to trap her.

In a motion almost too quick to follow, Jillian's foot lifted. He barely had time to avoid Fred's fate, and in jerking away from her, he gave her the room to wiggle free.

The mood in the room had altered. From jubilant anticipation of her quick defeat, now he could feel from his men his own reaction. She was good. Unorthodox and wily—and skillful.

He knew in that moment that he'd better drop all hesitation or she would embarrass him, too. She was sweating and breathing deeply, but her reflexes were still good, her movements limber. He'd better take her seriously.

A flare of triumph in her eyes told him that she knew she'd convinced him. He could stop the match now, but he'd better not, for her sake. His men resented her for embarrassing them in front of him.

He'd better either defeat her soundly or suffer their same fate. To walk away with this unfinished would help no one.

No way was Cullinane suffering their fate. He wasn't going to hurt her if he could help it, but for all of their sakes, he couldn't let her win.

She'd issued the challenge; now she had to live with the results.

Circling one another slowly, her gaze as intense as he felt, they jabbed and kicked, neither getting a decisive hit. Then he reached out to grasp her and bring this to an end—

And found himself flat on his back on the mat.

Cullinane reacted more quickly than she did, though. Her pause for the flash of a triumphant smile was one second too long. Before she could step out of range, he'd hooked one leg around her, dropping her to the mat, looming over her, the killing blow at her throat.

Around them the men recovered from the shock of her dropping him, exclamations of satisfaction coming from their throats.

But Cullinane heard no sound, too lost in the sudden stillness between them, too aware of her body beneath his, the roiling of his emotions too great. In seconds, he'd gone from chagrin to anger to triumph, and his control wavered, threatening to burst the bonds. Age-old instincts awakened—her slim throat beneath his hand, her hips all but joined to his, her fierce will to fight him drawing forth his own aggression. Watching her eyes darken, a surge of lust rocketed through him. He knew, in that moment, she could spell his destruction.

Jillian Marshall was more than dangerous. And he was doomed, if he didn't stay away.

Sitting back on his heels, still staring into her eyes, he slid his large hand from her throat, trailing it across one breast before standing up. She held his gaze, her chest rising with one quick indrawn breath, taut nipples outlined against her shirt. His hand burned like fire; his mind screamed for release—

He stood quickly, turning his back and walking away before he could make the biggest mistake of his life.

The room was utterly silent.

Jillian stretched under the hot water in her shower, remembering the moments after Cullinane had left the practice room. Head held high, she'd risen slowly from the mat, refusing to let them gloat. As she'd scanned the room, she'd been surprised to see reluctant admiration from the men lining the walls. Even Fred, with his cast, had nodded.

She'd lost, maybe more than she could bear to think about, but she'd gained their respect. Now if only she didn't have to think about those last moments with Cullinane.

Wincing at muscles she knew would be very sore tomorrow, she ducked her head under the water, hoping the impression of him would wash away, too. For those endless, naked moments, she'd felt what she knew he'd felt—a hunger too deep to forget.

She could still feel him over her, large hand at her throat, his fingertips burning a path across one breast. She'd wanted to part her legs and draw him into her, to drive her fingers into the long dark hair and bring his mouth to hers, to fight him and claw until he satisfied the need that kept building and building with every new encounter.

Jillian slapped both hands against the tile, shuddering at the image, the havoc it wreaked within her. It was wrong—*he* was wrong—she could not, *would not* feel this way any longer.

Then she snorted and shook her head, bringing her face full up under the pounding water, hoping to wash away his imprint. Damn him, damn him, damn him. How could any man make her feel this way?

But Cullinane wasn't any man. A chill settled into her bones, a cold fear that he could make her vulnerable, make her fail.

Flipping the control to Cold, Jillian shuddered, refusing to react to instinct and step away. If it took shocking her into her senses, by God, that's what she would do. She'd worked too hard, struggled too long, to let foolish fancies hold sway.

It was just hormones. For centuries, after the heat of battle, men and women had been celebrating life by making love. She might not be immune to biological imperatives, but it didn't mean she had to succumb. She'd known she risked much to challenge him—she'd just mistaken the nature of the cost.

Cold, rational thought, Jillian. No temper, no passion, no fancies. Admit that he makes your blood boil and move on.

Feeling better, Jillian stepped from the shower, and heard a knock at the door. "Who is it?"

"It's Alice, the housekeeper. Shall I come back?"

Thank God. A distraction. A human voice. "No, it's fine, just give me a minute." Hurriedly she slipped on a thick terry robe, then walked to the door, toweling her hair. Turning for the knob, she opened the door to a small woman with black, curly hair and a smile like Loretta's.

"I'm sorry if this is a bad time. I came to tidy your rooms."

"Sure, come in. I—will I be in your way?"

"Oh, no. I work around people all the time." With a cheery smile, the woman set down her carryall and pulled out a rag, moving to dust the furniture.

Jillian wasn't sure what to do with a housekeeper. Stay out of the way? Go back to her business? "Uh...I'll be in there." She pointed to the bathroom. "Let me know when you need me to move." Then she stopped and turned, heading toward the woman, holding out a hand. "I'm Jillian...Jillian Marshall. You're—Alice, did you say?"

Nodding, Alice seemed startled, then smiled and shook Jillian's hand. "Pleased to meet you, Jillian."

Her smile warmed Jillian. Such a little thing, but it made her realize how much she'd missed the little things. Small talk. Simple smiles. How did these people stand being cooped up in this place? They might as well be prisoners.

Eager to extend the pleasure, Jillian didn't leave, but trailed behind Alice.

The woman glanced up. "Can I help you with something?"

Jillian stepped back. "No...no, I was just—have you worked here long?" Oh, brother. Cullinane had probably made them all sign some secret pledge not to reveal anything to anyone.

Alice's smile was strained. "Three years. It's a

very good job for me. I have four children and no husband to help me.''

"Do you live far away?"

"No, I live on the grounds, in an apartment above the garage."

"Doesn't it—don't you get tired of it?"

Alice looked amused. "Of living in the countryside instead of the dump I could afford in the worst neighborhood in the city?" She shook her head. "No. My children are safe here, and they can attend good schools." A slight frown crossed her face, then her eyes filled.

"Are you all right?"

Alice glanced up. She shook her head, reached into her pocket for a tissue and blew her nose daintily. "I'm sorry. It's just that—"

"Please—" Jillian gestured to the chair nearby "—please sit down."

"I shouldn't—you can't—"

"Can't what? Can't listen?" It was wonderful to think about someone else's problems instead of her own. "Of course I can, if you'd like to talk." She tried another tack. "It must be very difficult, being a single parent."

Alice settled on the edge of the chair, glancing up gratefully, tears spilling over. "Oh, yes. Yes, it is." Her gaze looked stricken. "They're wonderful children, don't get me wrong."

"How many boys and girls?"

Alice brightened. "Two boys. My older one, J.T., is twelve." A shadow darkened her gaze for a moment, then she straightened, drawing a deep breath. "Adam, my other son, is nine. He looks up to J.T. so much.'' Again the sadness. ''I have two daughters, Lily, who is seven, and Mary Beth, my little one, just turned five.''

And J.T. is giving you trouble. ''A boy of twelve— it must be difficult, having no father to help with him.''

Alice's head rose, eyes troubled. ''He's a good boy, but lately…'' Alice shook her head, voice falling to a whisper. ''I thought this place would protect him, but I'm seeing odd things now. He's hanging around with some boys I don't know, boys with smart mouths and no respect. They always wear the same two colors.''

''Gang colors.''

The woman's eyes snapped to hers. ''I was hoping I was wrong. Are you sure?''

Jillian could have given her chapter and verse on gang behavior. Part of her time on the force had been working with gangs, trying to reverse the toll they were taking on the kids of San Diego. It had been the most frustrating part of her job.

But she could not afford any connections to her old life, so she merely nodded. ''I—I saw a television show recently, describing gang behavior. That's what's worrying you, isn't it?''

Alice's knuckles whitened, the grip of her hands was so tight. Head bowed, she nodded. ''I don't—he won't talk to me about it, and Adam…Adam will do anything he sees J.T. do. I—I don't want to lose either one of them, and I'm so worried. I thought we'd be safe here, so far from the old neighborhood.''

''It can't be hopeless yet.'' She would check out J.T., see what she could do.

Alice's head rose, her eyes shining. "Oh, I know it's not." She wiped at her eyes. "After all, there's Mr. Cullinane—"

"Cullinane?" What part did he play?

The woman nodded. "J.T. worships the ground that man walks on. I know Mr. Cullinane will help me." Rising to her feet, she began to dust again. "I don't know why I've talked so much. I—I'd better get this room done." Smiling shyly, she spoke over her shoulder, moving away. "I guess I've missed having other women to talk to."

Jillian let her pass without protest. She was still reeling over the concept of Cullinane as a substitute father. Mr. Granite? She hadn't observed the milk of human kindness exactly gushing from his veins. Shaking her head, she wanted to tell Alice to get herself and her kids away from this place, away from a monster like Hafner.

Did she know who he was? What he did?

"Alice, perhaps you shouldn't stay here if you think your children need to get away from bad influences around them. I know this place is nice, but room and board aren't enough."

Alice laughed, her laughter a clear, silvery tone that brought Jillian a smile. "Oh, I get much more than room and board. Klaus pays me very well for being his housekeeper, and he's started a college fund for each of my children. I have so few expenses that I'm able to put away quite a bit of my salary for that purpose, and he matches, two for one, every dollar I put away. In three years I've made a good nest egg for them." Her smile faded. "And my brother depends upon me. I couldn't leave."

Her brother? Jillian's head reeled from the thought that this kind, gentle woman was Hafner's sister, that Hafner would do such a generous thing. Then her words sank in. Three years. Alice had been here when Belinda was here.

He'd murdered Belinda. How could Alice not see what kind of man he was? What did she think had happened to Belinda? Could she not know Belinda was dead? Jillian felt she'd gone mad. How could this be the same man? College funds for Alice's children?

He'd done it, though. Killed Belinda. Her letters to Loretta, her calls—he'd intimidated her, kept her a virtual prisoner. She'd been terrified of him toward the end, and they'd been alone in that bayou cabin he'd used for a getaway. There was no doubt of it. He might support a whole orphanage, give money to the homeless, be the patron saint of a whole city, but he'd still murdered her sister—and others, by virtue of his livelihood. He was a merchant of death.

And Cullinane was the man he trusted most. Cullinane knew the answers.

But Jillian didn't dare ask. Not him, not even this sweet, harmless woman.

"Jillian? Ms. Marshall? Are you all right?"

Jillian's head snapped up, searching Alice's kind eyes. It was on the tip of her tongue to ask her if she'd met a woman named Belinda, but... Her shoulders sagged.

She was alone in this. She'd chosen this route. No secret ally would sweep in to help her. There were no shortcuts. She had to keep quiet, dig for information, look for her opportunity—and keep her wits about her.

Raising her head high and straightening her shoulders, she smiled calmly. "Yes. Yes, I'm fine. I'll leave you to your work."

And turned away, feeling more alone than when she'd opened the door.

Chapter Six

Late-afternoon shadows drifted across her bed. A knock sounded on her door, and Jillian stirred.

The knock came again, harder.

She sat up, muzzy from her nap. "Who is it?"

"It's Fred. Get up. Boss wants you."

Jillian shook her head, shoving her hair back out of her face. Rising slowly, muscles protesting, she scrubbed at her face with her hands and grabbed her robe from the end of the pale peach bedspread. "Just a minute…I'm coming."

Opening the door, she could see the signs of his disapproval, the smirk. Jillian straightened. "Yes?"

"Boss wants to go for a Sunday drive. Be ready in ten minutes." He held out her weapon. "Cullinane says you don't have to feel naked anymore." Fred's brown eyes glinted, and she fought the urge to hold her robe closer.

But she wouldn't give him the satisfaction. She took her weapon, meeting his gaze with chin lifted. "If you'll excuse me?" She started to close the door.

He shot out an arm to block it. For one instant she felt a frisson of fear.

The beefy blond man looked uneasy. Finally he blurted out, "You're…different."

She cocked her head, waiting. "Is that bad?"

He studied her carefully, shaking his head. "I don't know. You made me look bad," he said, glancing at his foot. "You shouldn't have been able to do that."

Jillian didn't know how to handle him, what to say. These men could make her life even harder if they wouldn't accept her. She didn't need any more obstacles. She stood quietly.

"Nobody's taken Cullinane down in a long time." He shifted uneasily on his feet, then glanced up, a slight grin curving his lips, and shrugged. "You might be all right."

Jillian grinned back, sighing inwardly with relief. "Thanks—Fred, right?" She glanced down at his foot. "I—I'm sorry about your foot. I'd been asleep. I didn't know what was—"

He waved off her words. "Forget it. It was the other guys laughing at me that hurt worse than anything. But after today, well, Cullinane beat you good, but that fall took the heat off me." With another grin, he stepped away, drawing the door closed. "Uh, the boss is waiting—"

She nodded and turned away, her heart a little lighter. Then she flew into action. She wouldn't give Cullinane a chance to chew her out for being late.

When she got downstairs, though, Cullinane was

nowhere in sight, and neither was the limo she'd ridden in the night they went to Algérie. In its place was a Ford Explorer, Hafner waiting at the passenger door.

"Would you do the honors and drive?"

Startled, Jillian frowned. "I don't know the area." *And I don't want to be alone with you.* No, that was wrong. That's exactly what she needed. Elation surged. Thank heavens, it wouldn't take forever, after all.

He waved a hand toward the driver's seat. "No matter. I do."

She shrugged. "You're the boss." But no time to plan, no strategy. Resolving to be vigilant for her opportunity, Jillian climbed into the seat, adjusting it to fit her.

Hafner settled into the seat beside her, then she heard the left rear door open and glanced in the mirror.

Cullinane.

Jillian ground her teeth in frustration. She should have known he would never let her do this alone. Glaring her challenge in the mirror, she met his gaze. "Perhaps Cullinane would rather drive? He does prefer to be in control, isn't that right, watchdog?"

The man of stone was back, full force. Black mane forbidding, the silver streak a warning. The man whose eyes had darkened with desire could have been a figment of her imagination. This man didn't evince even a grimace at the nickname.

Hafner laughed. "He does, indeed." Turning toward his security chief, he queried, "What do you say, Cullinane?"

Voice stony, Cullinane responded, "Just drive, Marshall."

Shadows dappled the driveway as she pulled away, Hafner giving directions. They headed farther out into the countryside. Jillian concentrated on her driving, trying desperately not to be unnerved by the presence of a man she loathed beside her—and the penetrating gaze that met her every time she glanced in the rear-view mirror.

When Hafner's arm stretched out to rest lightly on the top of her seat back, she steeled herself not to shift away.

Hafner rolled down the window, drawing in a deep breath of air filled with scents of decaying vegetation, exhaust fumes and the slowly settling heat of the day. "Ah, New Orleans suits me. I like the faint air of corruption that infuses everything." Turning toward her, he smiled, waiting for her reaction.

She glanced his way but said nothing, steering carefully. In the mirror, Cullinane's hard visage greeted her, but she couldn't read any expression there.

"Turn here, my dear." Hafner gestured. As their bodies swayed with the abrupt turn, his hand dropped to her thigh.

Jillian froze. Her glance shot up to the mirror to see if Cullinane saw it, but then she jerked her attention back quickly.

A squirrel darted across the road. Jillian barely missed it, Hafner's hand tightening on her thigh as the vehicle swayed.

She wanted to slap his hand away, to punch his

lights out. She wanted to bathe away his touch, even though her jeans barred him from touching her skin.

But she had a goal, a job to do. Hafner had to trust her to let her get close, again and again, until the opportunity presented itself. Tamping down her disgust, she gritted her teeth, glancing back in the mirror.

Cullinane's eyes burned her, his generous mouth set in a hard line, the flexing in his jaw condemning.

Jillian raised her chin and glared back.

"Pay attention, Marshall. There's a car following us."

Glancing in the mirror again, but past Cullinane, she saw he was right. She'd seen that car before, on the highway. *Focus, Jillian. Do this right.*

As she looked forward, a car drifted across the white line. She hadn't trained for evasive driving, not beyond what she'd learned at the academy. Her intelligence had said that Ron always drove Hafner everywhere.

A quick glance behind showed the car speeding up. The car in front hadn't corrected its angle; it was headed toward them.

"Get down, Klaus," Cullinane snapped. "Hit it, Marshall! See if you can get past them."

Jillian's fingers tightened around the wheel. She punched the accelerator, and the Explorer reacted quickly. The car in front speeded up, angling more.

"I can't make it," she said through gritted teeth. "I'm headed through those trees." Jerking the wheel hard, she prayed the vehicle wouldn't tip over as she ran it across the uneven ground.

A shot pinged the roof. She wanted to reach for her weapon, but steering took all her attention.

"Stay focused," Cullinane ordered. "Turn our side toward them when you have to stop."

She saw him edging toward the other door, gun ready. Aiming the Explorer at rougher ground where the cars behind them would have more trouble, she hoped she wouldn't have to slow down to shift into four-wheel drive. They were gaining slightly.

Suddenly a drop loomed. Too much to traverse, and solid cypresses at the base, the edge of the swamp too near. She wheeled the car around, leaving it running, and slid her weapon out of the holster. Cullinane slipped out of the back, gun drawn and ready.

A shot hit the rear window, but it didn't break.

"Bulletproof, thanks to my protector," Hafner said.

Jillian climbed past him. "Stay down. I'll see if I can help Cullinane."

When she got out, though, he was nowhere in sight. The black car that had been chasing them closed the gap. Jillian was crouched behind the wheel well, sighting in to shoot, when she was grabbed from behind, a hard blow to her arm knocking her weapon to the ground.

"Not bad, Marshall. Your evasive driving skills could stand some work, but at least you didn't panic."

Heart pounding she felt rage shoot through her body like a sniper's bullet. She jerked away and whirled, chest heaving. Angry words rocketed to her lips. With great effort, she swallowed them, adrenaline still pumping like quicksilver through her veins.

The cars behind them slowed and stopped. Ron and

two other men emerged. Hafner climbed out of the Explorer, grinning.

Only Cullinane looked displeased.

Hands on her hips, Jillian glared at him, angry words still fighting to escape from her lips. But she wouldn't give him the satisfaction. Turning insolently away from his regard, she leaned down and picked up her weapon, sliding it back into the holster.

"What did I tell you, Cullinane? Cool as a cucumber under pressure." Hafner's smug voice sounded. "She's ready—even you can't say she isn't." A taunting tone entered his next words. "I mean, any woman who can drop the unbeatable Cullinane..."

A grin crossed Ron's face. Jillian wished she were looking at Cullinane right now. Slowly she turned.

If looks could kill, she would be toast. She didn't care. This was sneaky, underhanded—

Effective. It had worked. Her final exam, and she'd passed it. She could see it in his gaze. He couldn't turn her away now. She smiled sweetly. "Do I get an A, teacher?"

His grim visage revealed nothing. Nodding at the men behind her, he snapped out an order. "Ron, you drive back. Check the Explorer—make sure there's no damage besides the window. Solly, you in front and the other car follows. Let's get back to the compound, people. Fun's over."

He started past her. Jillian shot out a hand to stop him. "Cullinane, admit it."

He towered over her, his closeness unsettling. The imperious eyebrow lifted. "Admit what?"

That I'm good, that I surprised you, that— Stop it, Jillian. You don't need this man's approval, you just need him to not interfere. She dropped her hand, shaking her head. "Never mind." As she walked toward the car, his voice stopped her.

"You're good, Marshall. That what you wanted to hear?"

She turned back. "But you don't like it."

His face hardened. "No. I don't. But I'm not paying the bills." He rounded the car.

Heart sinking, she chided herself for caring what he thought.

The drive back seemed to take hours.

Shirtless and barefoot, Cullinane watched her sleeping. Unable to sleep himself, he cursed her ability to drop off so easily.

But then, she'd had a very strenuous day.

He smiled faintly, then frowned. He couldn't send her away now. She'd proven herself; even he had to admit it. Hafner was jubilant, the other men accepting. Only Cullinane balked, with no other reason than his instincts to guide him.

But those instincts had kept him alive for a long time. He turned away from the monitor in disgust, wishing he could get a handle on what it was that bothered him so much about her.

Get real, Drake, he chided, one hand swiping at his hair. *She bothers you on every level.* He turned around to glare at the screen.

Jillian stirred and the sheet slipped down, drawing his gaze down with it, down to the nipple about to be revealed. He swore darkly, jabbing at the switch for that monitor, dissolving the image into darkness.

You can watch for the sake of security, but not because she sleeps naked.

But how could he wipe the image from his mind, prevent himself from dreaming it?

With a muffled curse he moved to his room, popping the buttons on his jeans and disrobing, then climbed into his own bed.

And tried not to wish he was climbing into Jillian's. The feel of the sheets against his skin maddened him, too reminiscent of how little separated them—only a little distance down the hall, only the bare covering of two sheets on their bodies...

Only a lifetime worth of hunting a killer.

Growling, Cullinane punched his pillow and flipped on his side, closing his eyes...

And praying for merciful oblivion.

Monday morning, the sun bright in the sky, Cullinane rapped impatiently at Hafner's door.

"Who is it, at this godforsaken hour?"

"It's ten o'clock, Klaus. Open up—we've got problems."

Too many moments passed. Cullinane was reaching for the knob when the door swung open onto Hafner's private lair. Cullinane barely registered the dark room, the sinister black-and-gold scheme. He thrust a sheaf of papers into Hafner's face.

Hafner blinked sleepily and frowned, running fingers through his short gray hair. "What's got you so riled up at this hour?"

"She's a liar. Jillian Marshall doesn't exist." Beginning to pace, he tried to still the thoughts swirling around in his head. He'd known it. He'd known something wasn't right. Now he'd proven it.

"So?"

Cullinane whirled in amazement. "So? You can ask me that, with this evidence? Have you lost your goddamn mind, Klaus? She's not who she says she is. She could be anyone, ATF, FBI, an assassin sent by some of your less well-meaning admirers—she's got to go."

"No."

Cullinane muttered a dark expletive. It wasn't likely she was any sort of government agent, but she could be working for someone who hated Hafner— God knew plenty of people did. If it weren't so serious, he would laugh. If he didn't believe in the soundness of his cover, he would almost think Hafner wanted to keep her just to confound him.

Frank's question returned to his mind, but did he dare question in that direction? *Had* Hafner brought her in to watch him?

Nonsense. She wasn't that good an actress. And he could almost swear he'd seen her respond to Hafner with revulsion.

Wouldn't it make more sense for her to seduce *him* if the goal was for her to watch him closely, to exert some control over him? But she'd fought him at every turn.

Cullinane felt every minute of his sleepless night. Running one hand over his face, he tried for patience. "You've never been like this since I've known you, Klaus. Tell me why you'd jeopardize everything for this woman."

"She intrigues me."

"She has the skills to kill you."

"Ah, but I have something she doesn't—you."

"I can't be with you every second. And that's where you're headed, anyway—to be alone with her. I can't protect you then."

Hafner straightened, his usual smug expression gone. "All right, Cullinane. I'll grant you that we don't know much about her—"

Cullinane snorted. "We know *nothing* about her, Klaus."

Hafner held his hands up, palms out. "That's not quite right. We know she's gutsy and has nerves of ice, she's strong and beautiful and smart. She's an uncommon woman, unlike anyone I've ever met— and I want to keep her around for a while." His tone was final. "I'll agree to avoid being alone with her until we can find out more about her, but I'm not sending her away. I trust your system, and, face it, Cullinane—we can watch her better here than outside. If she's really out to get me, she could do it anywhere. Let's keep her where we know what she's doing. There could be other reasons for her to be using an alias besides wanting to do me in. If she'd wanted that, why didn't she let me take a bullet yesterday? She didn't know it was a setup."

"I don't know—and I still don't like it."

"Objection noted." Hafner raised his gaze to Cullinane, his look almost fond. "I know you're just trying to do the job I hired you to do. You've done it damn well. Just give it some time, all right? So far, she's doing a great job."

Cullinane met his gaze evenly. "Don't go back on

your promise not to be alone with her, Klaus. Don't kid yourself—she's dangerous.''

Hafner nodded soberly. ''I know. It's part of the fascination.''

Cullinane retrieved the sheaf of papers. ''I'm going to figure out who she really is.'' Turning, he headed toward the door. When his hand gripped the knob, Hafner spoke.

''I'll agree the timing isn't great. I've got a big shipment coming in on the twenty-first, and there will be special arrangements.''

Cullinane's hand stilled on the knob. ''When do you want to go over them?''

''I don't have it all worked out yet, but soon. I'll need to work through part of it with you tomorrow, the rest later. There will be other players involved in this one.''

Hesitant to turn around for fear he would reveal his jubilation to Hafner, he nodded curtly. ''I'll be here.''

Then he left, more determined than ever to find the leverage to get Jillian Marshall or whoever the hell she was out of his life—quickly.

When Jillian finished her solitary lunch on the patio, Cullinane slipped up beside Alice as she carried the dishes into the kitchen. Removing the glass Jillian had used, holding it gingerly at the base with a napkin, he placed one finger against his lips and winked. Alice looked confused, but nodded.

Upstairs, Cullinane lifted the fingerprints carefully, slipping the white cards into a padded envelope. He would have to make a special contact to get the Bureau to run these, but he just couldn't shake the feeling that her true identity was important. Despite Hafner's willingness to gamble, Cullinane would not. Knockout redheads in black catsuits didn't just drop into your life for no reason. If nothing else, her timing was lousy. He didn't need any surprises right now.

He left the compound, headed for a pay phone. Whoever she was, he'd know soon.

On the way to his car he heard the voices of children chanting. Searching for the source, he spotted Alice's two girls playing jump rope—with Jillian. Or whoever she was.

Unbelievable.

Lily and Mary Beth were turning the rope while Jillian jumped, her cinnamon mane flowing in ribbons with each leap. Caught by the sight of her, he stopped, her wide smile compelling his own, her laughter musical and inviting.

Then she saw him and missed a step. Stopping, she laughed, her head tilted in curiosity. Realizing his own smile had triggered it, he sobered. When her face fell, he had a sense of something intimate lost.

She's a liar, Drake. Pulling his gaze away from hers, abruptly saddened, he got into his car and drove away, more disturbed than ever.

He was a liar, too. Maybe her reasons were as good as his own.

Frowning, Jillian watched him drive away.

"What's wrong, Jillian? You can have another turn," Mary Beth offered. "We don't have to count it."

"What?" Jillian pulled her gaze away from the car

driving off. "Oh—no, that's all right, sweetie. I'm a little winded, anyway. It's Lily's turn now, right?"

Lily, though older, was shyer than her sister. She flushed, then handed her end to Jillian. She waited patiently for Jillian and Mary Beth to get their rhythm going before jumping in, but Jillian was finding concentration hard to command.

He'd smiled at her, actually smiled. She would have to admit that she'd admired those generous lips before, accentuated by the cleft in his chin. But they were always set in resistance to her, so hard and often angry. She thought she was almost glad now. That smile was deadly.

Lily stumbled, and Jillian dragged her thoughts back quickly, dropping the rope so the girl wouldn't get tangled up and fall.

"Mama?" The girl glanced back at her mother, fear washing her face.

"I see him, honey." Alice opened the kitchen door and stepped out, face hard as she looked toward the compound gate.

Jillian turned to see what it was. Two boys, one short and wiry, his whole demeanor shouting "attitude." A larger boy strutted beside him. Mary Beth slipped her hand into Jillian's.

The larger boy scanned Jillian with eyes much too old for a face that was years from needing a razor.

"J.T., you come in now. You've got homework to do," Alice ordered.

The two boys exchanged looks. Mary Beth's hand squeezed Jillian's.

"In a little while." J.T.'s surly tone grated on Jillian's nerves. If his mother hadn't been there, she would have liked to peel a strip off his hide, take him down a notch. But these weren't her children.

Alice's voice shook slightly. "Rabbit needs to go home now. You can play later."

The larger boy snorted, turning away. "Yeah, sure, mama's boy." His tone slid into singsong. "You can find someone to *play* with when your homework is done. Maybe after the milk and cookies are gone. I'm outta here." With an arrogant wave, he strolled back to the gate, whistling.

J.T. flushed, shooting his mother a look of naked hatred. Jillian could see the woman recoiling. Uncomfortable witnessing it, she busied herself with the girls.

"Okay, girls, why don't you go inside and wash your hands before your snack? Here, Lily, take Mary Beth." The older girl stepped away from her mother and did as Jillian asked.

Alice dropped her head, shoulders sagging. "I should take them somewhere, get away from this place. But Klaus—"

"Why doesn't he help you with them?"

The woman's voice went quiet. "I don't like to bother him with my problems. He's a busy man, and I know the children's noise sometimes bothers him. I don't want to make too much trouble—I'm already beholden to him as it is." She turned to walk away.

"Alice? Do you want me to talk to J.T. for you?"

The woman turned back, pale blue eyes brimming with unshed tears. "No, it's not your problem." Shuttering her gaze, Alice steadied her voice. "I have to learn how to take care of it myself. They're my children."

"Something wrong, Alice?" Jillian turned at the voice. Hafner's demeanor was icy, his face hard.

Alice grasped the door handle, her face losing all animation. "No, Klaus, everything's fine." Quickly she scooted inside, face pale.

Jillian frowned at the odd exchange. When Alice shut the door behind her, Jillian turned away.

Hafner grabbed her arm. Heart thudding, she stepped back, but Hafner held on.

"I've been looking for you." He slipped one arm around her waist. His voice fell to an intimate tone. "I need you tonight."

Jillian froze, every nerve screaming for her to run.

Chapter Seven

Hafner gazed down at her. "I have clients to entertain."

Relief flooded her, followed by chagrin. She had to get past revulsion with him, if she were to succeed. She wasn't there yet.

"What troubles you?" He reached out to smooth the skin between her eyebrows.

Jillian recoiled, stepping away. "Nothing. I'd—I'd better go get ready. What's the dress tonight?"

He smoothed his palm along her arm.

It was all she could do not to shudder.

Gazing deeply into her eyes, he squeezed her elbow in his large, warm hand. "Dress to the nines, Jillian. Let me see one of my new pretties on your lovely body."

She stood very still, fighting the urge to jerk away. "What time?"

"Seven. You might want to rest a little first. It will be a long night. I want to dance with you, Jillian. I want to hold your body against mine."

Swallowing hard, feeling like a butterfly on a pin, she straightened, willing herself to calm. "I'll be ready."

But she'd never be ready for him to touch her.

"Jillian," he called out. She didn't turn. "I can be very good to you, if you'll let me."

With all the dignity she could muster, she walked away slowly, when what she really wanted was to run.

"Jillian." Cullinane spoke out across the dinner table. "I can't quite place your accent."

She shrugged lightly, then glanced away. "I've lived a lot of places."

"Where is your family now?"

"My father's dead." Sadness pervaded her voice.

He wanted her to squirm, but not this way. "I'm sorry. Your mother's alone?"

"She left when I was very young." To her credit, she held his gaze steadily.

"Where was she from?"

"Is this a dinner party, Cullinane, or an interrogation?" Hafner drawled out.

The others at the table tittered. Jillian looked away, smiling at Hafner.

"Just interested in your new companion, Klaus." He toyed idly with his wineglass, running a lazy finger around the edge. "Just making conversation."

Jillian looked up as though something in his tone alerted her. There was an unnatural brightness to her gaze tonight, almost a desperation.

The band began its first set. Klaus stood, holding out a hand to Jillian. ''I believe you promised me a dance, my dear.''

The feverish look flared. Jillian glanced over at him. Cullinane shrugged his shoulders negligently. What did she expect him to do, when she'd already promised Klaus a dance? He didn't care what she did, as long as she didn't foul up his operation.

But he watched them. The long meal had taken its toll, having to watch Jillian across the expanse of snowy white cloth, seeing that damned short red sequined dress, knowing how long her legs were, though hidden beneath the table—

Hell. He shifted in his seat, looking around the table to see if there was anyone he wanted to ask to dance with him.

There wasn't.

His gaze returned to Jillian, her body held close against the length of Hafner's. Too close. But she was a cool customer, her face a mask of icy unconcern.

Cullinane stood, turning to the woman next to him. ''Care to dance?''

Startled, she nodded. He held out a hand, knowing from her expression that Mrs. What's-Her-Name likely thought she would be dancing with the devil. He forced himself to smile and make small talk, moving into an easy rhythm to help her get over her nerves. She barely reached halfway up his chest, so he had a clear shot to watch what he really wanted to see.

Jillian.

The short red dress followed the lines of her body, the fringe softly swaying with each move, tiny sparkles glinting red fire. Her long burnished hair swept against pale skin—hair that had brushed his cheek only a few nights before.

He remembered the feel of her body against his, the clean apple scent of her hair, the warm sigh of her breath against his throat…the silken texture of her skin.

Hafner's fingers slipped between the low back of her dress and that same skin. Cullinane's jaw clenched. When they turned, Cullinane could see deep unease in her eyes.

Damn it, Jillian. Marshall. Whoever you are.

"Is something wrong?" his partner asked timidly.

"What?" He glanced down, seeing her brow wrinkled. "Oh—no, nothing. Just a stray thought." He smiled to put her at ease.

The woman couldn't hold his gaze long. As soon as she looked away, he glanced back. Hafner's arm had wrapped all the way around Jillian's back, pulling her into him, the fingers of one hand stroking near her breast.

Cullinane went rigid. "I'm sorry." He interrupted his partner. "I—I forgot something I have to take care of. Will you please excuse me?"

Cullinane walked her back to the table, bowing over her hand and assuring her that he would like another dance later, if that were possible. Excusing himself, he returned to the dance floor, headed straight for Hafner and Jillian, pressure building inside him.

She spotted him, her expression a mixture of anger and relief. Sensing her motion, Hafner turned, frowning.

"What's up?"

"I'm not sure. I need Marshall to check the exterior with me." He saw Hafner's hands rest on Jillian's hips.

"What about Ron and Tony?"

His teeth clenched. "Ron's down the block. Tony's the one who asked for help."

Hafner looked exasperated. "Can't you handle it by yourself?"

He leveled a gaze at Hafner, instead of the blow he'd like to level at his head. "You asked me to be in charge of security, Klaus. Now let me do my job."

Hafner studied him for a long moment, then nodded. "I'll make your excuses. Perhaps Jillian needs a little fresh air, and of course, I can't leave my guests."

Cullinane nodded impatiently. "That should work." Turning to Jillian, he gestured with his head. "Ready?" He had to keep his hands off her, especially now, when his temper threatened.

Her cool demeanor was back, except for a faint light of gratitude in her gaze, mixed with equal parts of wariness. She nodded.

Looking down on the pale skin at the part of her hair, he thought she seemed somehow vulnerable. Cullinane placed one hand at her back protectively, walking out beside her. He drew in a sharp breath at the contact. Touching her was definitely a mistake.

"What's wrong?"

"Shh, not in here." He led her outside, head swiveling, spotting a shadowed corner in the rear of the building, deserted.

They reached the corner, where moonlight and shadows interfaced. "What are we looking for?"

He spun her around, pushing her up against the building, trapping her hands at shoulder level with his own, his body settling against hers as he struggled with the last remnants of his detachment. In the shifting moonlight he could still see her eyes widen, her lips part slightly, her breasts rising above the sparkling fabric with every breath. Fringe shimmered with her every movement, outlining the curves his hands ached to touch. He could still see Hafner's hands on her. He had to erase them, imprint himself.

Cullinane leaned closer. Jillian gasped. Her breasts rubbed against his chest, the contact shooting sparks through his body. He sucked in a breath, struggling for the control to walk away. This was crazy. He shouldn't want to mark her as his.

But he did.

"Trouble, Jillian. That's what we're looking for. Trouble, pure and simple." His mouth descended toward lips he'd hungered to taste for far too long. He paused just a breath shy of them, giving her a last chance to move away.

But Jillian moaned, a soft, feminine sound—and then it was too late.

Hot, edgy need shot through him, a craving like nothing he'd ever felt. He didn't want to want her, but it was beyond him now. Dark...angry...voracious—need tore away his iron control. He had to have more of her. He needed everything, everything she had.

Dropping her wrists, he slid his arms around her, drawing her closer, hating the boundaries of clothing and skin. Drowning…he was drowning, losing all concept of who he was and where they were, craving her with everything in him.

Lost. Jillian was lost, she was helpless, dying from want of this man. Her senses stolen by the unexpected turn, Jillian couldn't fight him. Didn't want to.

Hafner's hands on her had disgusted. Cullinane's hands stole her mind. Desperate to draw closer, she drove her fingers into his dark mane, almost knowing when she touched the silver streak. Her fingers slid through cool satin, clawed against warm flesh.

He shifted, parting their mouths for a split second. She whimpered, pulling him back. He took her deeper—hot, clever tongue swirling and luring, tempting her further into madness.

Oh, but such a fine madness it was. He stole her breath, the feel of his hard body so welcome against her. When he pulled away to tease a burning path down her neck, her knees gave way, his arms all that held her up. His mouth fastened on the tender flesh where neck and shoulder met; he sucked gently, then nipped lightly—and goose bumps broke out over her whole body.

She sighed, and Cullinane chuckled, lifting her higher in his arms, feet off the ground as he licked a long, sinuous stroke over the curve of her breast, her nipples aching for his mouth.

She was a heartbeat from wrapping her legs around his waist and begging when the crunch of gravel sounded nearby. Voices rang out, coming closer. In seconds they would be seen.

She stiffened, hearing Cullinane inhale sharply. He groaned softly, letting her down with care, drawing her deeper into the shadows. His chest heaved, his eyes glittering with need. He looked as shell-shocked as she felt.

"God, I—" Confusion warred with anger in his gaze, but nowhere could she see the stoic man she knew.

Jillian placed two fingers on his lips, a movement behind them catching her eye. "It's Tony. He doesn't see us yet." She couldn't look at him again, couldn't explain what had just happened. Stepping away, she struggled to compose herself, turning her back on the man who'd just rocked the foundations of her world. "I'll head that way—" she nodded toward the left "—and do what you told Hafner we were going to do." *And try to recover my mind.*

"Jillian…" His voice was rough, unsteady.

"Don't—please." Aching for him, she turned back. The forbidden stranger was already returning, but his eyes hadn't hardened yet. "I don't—this was just—" She shook her head, having no idea what it was, what to call what had happened. It was too deep, too raw for words.

"A mistake," his grim voice intoned.

She knew he was right, but that didn't stop it from hurting.

Nodding curtly, he turned away. "I'll go this way, then rejoin Hafner. Get Tony to drive you home."

Home. Jillian wanted to laugh. Instead, she picked up the purse she'd dropped and walked away on unsteady legs.

Once she'd left, Cullinane walked around the building, nodding at Tony. "Marshall's checking a disturbance out back. Take her to the compound when she makes it to the front. We'll be along soon.''

The man nodded. ''Sure thing.''

Barely aware of where he was or what he was doing, Cullinane scrambled to make his insides match the mask he'd struggled to paste over gut-wrenching turmoil. Stopping inside before going to meet Hafner, he moved toward a pay phone and picked up the receiver, buying time to get a grip on what had just happened.

Are you insane, Drake? He shook his head. *What was that all about?*

You want her. Badly. You hate seeing Hafner all over her.

All of it was true, but none of it mattered. All that mattered, all that *could* matter, was the operation. So close—too close to screw up now. But he was still shaking inside from the impact of the experience. No woman had ever hit him that hard.

He had to remember that she'd lied to him. Was still lying, every time she answered to the name Jillian Marshall.

He'd never made love to a phantom woman before.

And he wouldn't. Couldn't. No matter that he still wanted her with every breath in his body, that he ached for her even now.

Rubbing temples that felt squeezed in a vise, he shook off his thoughts and straightened, disregarding the odd look of the maître d'.

Crossing the crowded floor in long strides, he spotted Hafner's table. As if feeling his glance, Hafner looked up, a frown crossing his face. Rising and laying down his napkin, Hafner murmured to his guests, then approached.

"What are you doing here? Where is Jillian?"

"I sent her back."

Hafner shot him a look of challenge. "Why?"

"Her job tonight was finished. I can handle it from here."

"I say when she's finished, Cullinane." Hafner's voice rose, attracting attention.

"Keep your voice down."

Hafner's eyes sparked. "Don't tell me what to do—I pay your salary, damn it. You bring her back now."

"No, Klaus."

A feral gleam lit his gaze. "It's her, isn't it? You want her. You can't stand the thought that she's mine for the taking. You're jealous."

Jaw clenched, Cullinane struggled for calm. "She's no one's for the taking." But it was true—he was jealous, jealous as hell, and crazy to feel it.

Hafner's eyes narrowed. "If I say she's mine, she's mine."

"She's not a hooker, she's a bodyguard."

"Goddamn it, Cullinane," Hafner roared, "I want her here now."

Cullinane grabbed his arm, jerking him toward the alcove leading to the rest rooms. Once out of sight, he yanked Hafner up by the lapels. "Shut up, you fool. She's not a bitch in heat, and you're not her master. Now leave her alone to do her job. If you can't keep your zipper closed around her, I'll have her off the property so fast your head will spin, do you hear me?"

"Don't threaten me, Cullinane," the low voice warned. "Not even you can threaten me."

Watch it, Drake. You're out of control. He was walking a thin line, disaster yawning ahead. Drawing a deep breath, he loosened his fingers from the fabric, setting Hafner away from him but never breaking the stare. "You're losing sight of your business, Klaus. You're letting those long legs keep you from thinking straight. Maybe that's what someone wants to have happen, ever think of that?"

He could see the moment when temper turned into comprehension. Hafner's stance eased, and he chuckled, shaking his head.

Cullinane's own body still twanged with tension.

Hafner smiled the smile of a predator. "Damn fine legs, though, don't you agree?" Cocking his head, he probed Cullinane's gaze warily. "I still think you want her as much as I do." Clapping one hand to Cullinane's shoulder, he smirked. "Nice to know my stone-faced protector is human." He turned to go back, then stopped suddenly and whirled, pointing a finger, eyes hard and determined. "She's mine, though, if I want her—remember that. Nobody touches her but me."

Cullinane stood there for a moment, watching him walk away.

Get out, Jillian, while you still can. You need protection from both of us.

Jillian stood in the moonlight, staring off in the distance, seeing nothing. She'd circled the parking lot perfunctorily, her mind roiling in confusion, her body still thrumming like a plucked string. Unmet need clawed at her, yet her mind screamed in anger.

Fool. Idiot. Weakling. From the first, he'd exerted a potent allure, a magnetism that had drawn her steadily closer to the flame. Just like a sorcerer practicing black magic, he seemed to draw from something deep within her, something she had no idea how to kill. She'd thought she'd done well at suppressing it, but tonight, in seconds, it had roared to life like a forest fire consuming acres of ground in a flash.

She didn't know what to do except stay away from him as much as possible. Anger hadn't helped, icy disdain made no impression. Whatever it was within her that sought its match in him was beyond anything she'd ever tried to control before.

But she had to. Before she had no other choice but to leave.

And live the rest of her life with the guilt.

"Jillian?" Tony stepped forward. "I called you twice."

"Oh, sorry. I—never mind."

He looked at her oddly. "Something wrong? Something I need to check out?"

She shook her head. "No, it's nothing."

Studying her face, he hesitated. "Cullinane told me to drive you back. You ready?"

No, I'm not ready for any of this. I thought I was, but I'm scared. Scared it's all spiraling out of my control. Scared I'm about to fail.

She lifted her chin, wrapping the remnants of icy control around her. "Yeah, I'm ready. Let's go."

She'd whistle past the graveyard until she could figure out how to disarm Cullinane's most potent weapon.

Himself.

Chapter Eight

Hafner lounged against the black leather sofa, tie off, shirt half-unbuttoned. Waving negligently with the glass in his hand, he indicated the bar on the near wall. "Have a drink, Cullinane." Nudging the ornate wooden box on the smoked-glass tabletop with the foot propped next to it, he smiled expansively. "How about a cigar?"

"No, thanks, Klaus. I'm ready to turn in."

"You ever a Boy Scout, Cullinane?" Hafner studied him through spirals of smoke.

Cullinane smiled. For a man ready to go several rounds in the restaurant earlier, Hafner showed no signs now that he'd ever been ruffled. "My neighborhood was a little short on the amenities."

"Mine, too." Hafner looked into his drink, swirling the dark liquid. "I'll never go back." Raising eyes glittering with repressed emotion, he gestured around the room. ''My whole house could have fit in this room.''

Cullinane nodded. His, too. ''So you weren't a Boy Scout, either?''

Hafner chuckled. ''Lifting wallets was a little more my speed, at that age.'' His gaze rose to Cullinane's. ''Or feeling up girls.''

The atmosphere thickened, as two dominant males remembered a clash that evening, better left unexplored. Cullinane held his gaze, knowing a lot was on the line at this moment. Hafner's respect for him had come because the man couldn't bully him. Cullinane yielded when he wanted to yield, both of them sidestepping any full confrontation. He suspected Hafner didn't want to find out that he might not win.

Hafner broke the gaze, leaning his head back on the overstuffed cushion, sliding lower in his seat and closing his eyes. ''Let's talk about the next shipment.''

So typical of him. He slept little and expected those around him to keep his erratic hours. The middle of the night was high noon for him, a man who'd gotten soft letting others guard him, who'd lost the sharp physical edge he'd once used as a weapon. Cullinane and his men had to keep their bodies honed, and that meant rest and proper care. Hafner forgot that when the night specters beckoned.

Moving to a nearby chair, Cullinane sat down. ''What's up?''

''It's going to be trickier than usual. Some of the boats will be coming in with specialty items I don't usually carry, along with the coke. We'll need to set up carefully to off-load the coke but not disturb the other stuff, just finish filling those boats with part of the outgoing shipment.''

''What kind of specialty items?''

Hafner's sly smile made his scalp crawl. ''Nerve gas canisters.''

Cullinane barely blinked, carefully masking his inner shock. ''You're planning, of course, to help load those particular boats.''

A wide grin creased Hafner's face, then he laughed out loud. ''I can't shock you, can I, watchdog?'' He shook his head, amusement still lighting his gaze. ''Never let 'em see you sweat, do you, Cullinane?''

He couldn't believe Hafner was serious, but he had to be sure. More calmly than he felt, he pressed. ''You really think our people are prepared to handle them?''

''They'd better be, but that's part of your job. You make sure we have what we need.''

''I'll need figures on quantity and space required.''

Hafner nodded. ''I'll get them to you tomorrow or the next day.''

He was really going to do it. The man was insane. Not only was the stuff lethal, but he would get the book thrown at him if he were caught.

And he would be caught this time. Cullinane would make sure of it. Sure that he locked Hafner up and threw away the key himself.

But the man had just upped the ante on this operation. They would need expert handling at the shipment site.

Cullinane met the gaze of a madman, a man wily as a fox but dangerous as they came. For all that he seemed human, he lacked an essential element to make him care. The lives of most other human beings meant nothing to him and his ilk.

Slapping his palms down on his thighs, Cullinane rose. "Well, I'm calling it a day. Unless you have something else?"

Hafner studied him for a moment, smiling oddly. "Jillian is lovely, isn't she?"

He held the gaze steadily, refusing to rise to the bait. "Yeah," he responded, daring Hafner to press.

Hafner's smile was at odds with the gleam in his gaze. "Sweet dreams, watchdog."

Words unspoken passed between them.

"I'm sure they will be. Good night." He turned and left.

Jillian heard the fight break out in the game room the next day. Headed down the hall to see why J.T. and Rabbit were going after each other, she'd almost turned the corner when she heard the deep voice cut through the fracas like a hot knife through butter.

She couldn't hear the words, but Rabbit's protesting tone came through, loud and clear, followed by J.T.'s own. Cullinane's tone of command stopped them before they could get rolling again.

Rabbit's sullen shout echoed. "Fine, just fine—I'm outta here."

Stepping back into the library next door, Jillian saw him rush past, face screwed up in anger. Before she could make her way back into the hall, she heard Cullinane and J.T. headed her way.

She hadn't seen him at all that day; he'd even

changed his workout time to avoid her. He wasn't likely to want to see her now.

J.T.'s voice quavered. "I'll show him who's bad."

"Are you so sure you can't talk it out?" Cullinane asked.

Jillian's mouth dropped open. Mr. Granite said that? Mr. My-Way-or-the-Highway was talking compromise?

"He'd never listen. He only understands fighting."

"Fighting rarely solves anything, J.T. There's usually a better way."

J.T.'s skepticism came through in his tone. "I never thought I'd hear you say something soft like that."

Cullinane chuckled. "There's nothing wrong with being soft sometimes."

Jillian sat down before she could fall down.

"You're never soft, Cullinane."

Sadness crept into his voice. "I'm not saying I'm any example to follow, J.T. The best man I ever knew was strong enough to be soft sometimes."

"Was that your dad?"

"No. It was my grandfather. I never knew my dad."

"I did, but mine don't care what happens to me. He left us a long time ago, after Mary Beth came." His voice fell, his tone confiding. "I was too much trouble."

"I don't think it was you, J.T. Maybe he cares. Sometimes people just make mistakes. He'd care if he saw you now."

"I wouldn't give that creep the time of day."

"Then that's your loss, and his, too. But you can't

live your life looking back over your shoulder.
You've got to go on from where you are now. And
where you are, J.T., is that your mother needs you.
She's taken care of all of you by herself for a long
time now. You're older. You need to be helping her,
not hanging out with losers like Rabbit.''

"Rabbit's no loser. He can beat anybody around.''

"That's not the measure of a real man.''

"Then what is?''

"A real man takes care of his responsibilities, tries
not to let down those who care about him, those he
cares for.''

Jillian held her breath, hearing in those words
something deep within the man himself.

But who did Cullinane care for? Who cared for
him? She'd never met a more solitary man. Knowing
that, and hearing his words, gave her a deeper understanding of the somber shadows she'd sensed.

"I can't make much money to help my mom. I'm
only twelve.''

"Money isn't the key. What your mom needs is
for you to help her guide the younger ones. Adam
watches every move you make, and the girls need
your guidance, too. Haven't you noticed that they're
afraid of Rabbit and of how you act when you're with
him?''

"No, I—I never thought about it.''

"Let me tell you something, J.T. When I was your
age, I was the baddest dude around. So puffed up with
my swagger and how nobody could tell me nothin'
about nothin'.''

Jillian smiled as his cadence brought the vision of
a young, dark-haired wild boy to life in her mind.

"Yeah?" J.T.'s tone held the gleam that must be in his eyes.

"Yeah. You think that sounds great, right?" Cullinane's tone hardened. "Well, let me tell you something. I almost got my best friend killed with my swaggering because I was like Rabbit, too mixed up in my head to see the dead end I was walking down. And like you, I was mad at the whole world because I'd been given a rough turn. I had no dad, I lived in a shack and nobody cared if I lived or died except one old man."

His tone grew quiet. "They hauled my best friend to the hospital, bleeding from a stab wound that hit almost too close to his heart in a fight with some guys I wouldn't back down from. The cop who brought me home told my grandfather that he'd be smart to let them take me into foster care. He said I'd never be anything but misery for him."

Jillian found herself leaning forward.

"So what did your grandfather do?"

"First he blistered my butt so hard I couldn't sit down until the next afternoon."

"And then?"

"And then he hugged me. Hugged me so hard I could barely breathe. And he told me something I've never forgotten."

"What?"

"Sometimes the strongest person is the one who walks away."

In the silence that followed, Jillian could hear the cracking of her heart. It was difficult to believe that she was hearing the same hard, angry man who was so determined to get rid of her.

But the compassion she heard in his voice as he reached out to a troubled boy was another face of a complex man. A man of deep feelings, hidden by a very tough shell.

A shell that had cracked open last night long enough to singe her to her toes.

A complex man, indeed. Jillian shook her head, fingers pressed to her lips, wishing she hadn't heard this conversation. It only made it harder to stay away.

"You, uh, you think I should stay away from Rabbit, huh?"

"No. I don't—not necessarily."

"You don't?"

"You have to make your own decisions, J.T. That's part of becoming a man. But remember that who you surround yourself with is a measure of who you are and who you want to be. Make your choices count." She heard him start to walk. "But for now, how about choosing to shoot some hoops with me in the gym?"

"Yeah!" No more world-weary tones from J.T. His steps picked up speed.

And then they were gone, leaving Jillian to wonder who this man really was. *"Who you surround yourself with is a measure of who you are and who you want to be."*

Remember that, Jillian. He's here, with the man who killed your sister.

She rose slowly from the chair and left the room, her mind awhirl.

Jillian walked into the gym early the next morning, angry and raw with fatigue from a night wasted on useless confusion. The man who stood most squarely in the way of a goal she had to accomplish had interfered with her sleep, as well.

Tossing and turning, she'd wished for nothing more than to have met Cullinane another place, another time. He fascinated her like a Chinese puzzle ring, one that seemed hopeless to solve but somehow fit smoothly together. She'd seen the smooth exterior, but it was the jumble underneath that held her interest.

Doing her stretches, Jillian shook her head, angry and disturbed and sad. She didn't understand him—and couldn't afford to try.

So why couldn't she just forget him and get on with the task at hand?

Because the task you set yourself is not going according to plan.

She'd never counted on it taking so long. She'd never planned to meet Alice and wonder what would happen to her and her four children if Hafner died. She'd never counted on Cullinane.

And that might be the most deadly omission of all.

He protected an amoral killer, yet he kissed her with a passion that set her every nerve on fire. He taunted and tested her at every turn, doing everything in his power to break her—yet he helped a confused young boy off the path to destruction with a firm, gentle hand.

Jillian balled up her T-shirt and threw it at her reflection in the mirror, resisting the urge to scream in frustration. It floated to the floor, as ineffectual as she herself had been so far.

"What are you doing here, Jillian?" she asked her reflection.

"I'd be interested in the answer," Cullinane's deep voice replied.

She jumped, her gaze zooming to where he stood filling the doorway.

"What *are* you doing here, Marshall?"

Shaking her head slightly, she moved away. "It seems obvious, since I'm in the gym." Raising her gaze to his, she scanned his sweat-soaked T-shirt. "You're ahead of me this morning."

"I decided to run first." *So I'd miss meeting you here.*

Drake thought Jillian looked tired, not her usual spunky self. He wondered if her nights were as sleepless as his. He hoped so. He didn't want to be the only one off balance.

Not meeting his eyes, she walked away, climbing onto the stair stepper. He thought about going back outside or skipping his workout altogether. But he couldn't avoid her forever. He'd faced down cold-blooded killers with less trepidation than he felt seeing her again after losing his mind in her arms.

Now watching her from the rear, seeing those long legs in motion—he jerked away, turning to scan the room. *Work. Sweat her out if you have to. But get this obsession with her out of your mind.*

Damning the mirrors yet again for making it too easy to see her from anywhere in the room, he went to the floor to do push-ups. He was safe from her reflection while he was staring at the floor.

Jillian focused on the mirrors in front of her, trying to look anywhere but at the powerful ropes of muscles in his arms and across his back. His already-wet shirt clung like a second skin, revealing the ripple of muscles as though he were naked.

She closed her eyes and climbed, digging for the anger that had protected her in the beginning. She wished she'd never heard his conversation with J.T. She didn't want to know that he could be gentle, that he could be soft. She wanted to remember the man of stone, the hardened warrior—anything to keep her on target.

Anger simmered within her, and she nursed it like the only flame in a world of winter, begging it to keep her alive, in tune with her mission.

When she found herself watching him again, she jammed a finger on the panel, setting the pace higher. *Good. You're not pushing hard enough if you have energy to think.* That was the answer—she would work until she dropped, and push to find a way to get Hafner alone, very soon.

And get out of this place before Cullinane makes you forget why you're here at all.

Time passed in silence. Cullinane had studiously avoided looking at her, working his way through each set of reps with the concentration of a drone, the precision of a machine, trying to forget she was in the same room—

Until he heard her soft moan of distress.

Glancing up, he found he already knew exactly where she was, and crossed to her quickly.

"Give it to me," he ordered, standing behind her and lifting the bar out of her hands. Setting it carefully in the rack, he looked back down to see her facing him, hands on hips, eyes bright with anger.

"I didn't ask you to do that," she snapped.

"If you'd had any sense at all, you'd have asked me to spot you."

"I don't want your help."

He stepped closer, inches away. "That's obvious. What the hell are you doing, upping the weight that much?"

"How do you know I've upped it?"

"I notice a lot of things about you, Jillian." His voice went husky against his will.

"Don't," she retorted, turning away.

"Don't what?"

Her eyes looked at him in the mirror, anguished and confused. "Just—don't." She looked away, stepping back under the frame and beginning to reach for the bar again.

"What are you doing?"

"It's obvious," she snapped. "I'm finishing my set."

"Take off some plates."

"Leave me alone." She grasped the bar firmly, preparing to lift it off the rack.

"Don't do it, Jillian." He couldn't interrupt her motion once she started. She would definitely hurt herself.

"Get out of my way."

He stood right behind her, ready to catch it. "You're not doing this alone." Their gazes met in the mirror, and he softened his tone. "If you insist on doing that extra weight, I want to help you."

She didn't answer, but he saw the concession in her eyes. Keeping the smallest distance between them that would still allow her to lower herself into the squat, he fitted his body to hers like spoons in a drawer, mirroring her every action, arms out and ready to catch the bar if she faltered.

With slow, steady motion downward, she bent, her behind brushing the air so close to his loins that he hardened in an instant. Their bodies fit together as though made to be a set.

Carefully he watched her every movement, letting his body follow hers in the rhythm she set, molding himself to her as if half of one whole.

Jillian could barely concentrate on isolating her muscles, so aware was she of the feel of him at her back. Yet somehow they fell into sync, Cullinane matching her motions so perfectly that she felt strengthened by his presence, safe and protected.

When her muscles screamed at the burn, she stopped, ready to lift the bar up and onto the rack. But strong arms took the burden from her, setting it above her head, then those same strong arms pulled her back against his hard chest.

For a moment that seemed eternal they stood there facing the mirror together, Cullinane's powerful arm wrapped around her waist, holding her to him like a woman cherished. His once-steely eyes were alive with pain and promise, fixed on her face as though looking for answers to questions as tortured as her own.

His fingers spread across her ribs, his thumb grazing the lower curve of her breast. She could see her nipples peak in the glass before her; she could feel him harden behind her. Heat shimmered in the air around them, wrapping them in a web of longing, casting them under his sorcerer's spell.

THE READER SERVICE™
FREEPOST CN81
CROYDON
SURREY
CR9 3WZ

If the offer card is missing write to: The Reader Service, P.O. Box 236, Croydon, Surrey CR9 3RU.

NO
STAMP
NEEDED IF
POSTED IN
THE U.K.
OR N.I.

She'd never seen a sight more erotic. Or more frightening. Stirring, she tried to move away.

He held her fast. "Don't, Jillian. Just give us this moment."

For what? What good would it do? They were ever at odds, ever would be. There was no meeting ground between them.

"Look at us, Jillian. Tell me it doesn't make your blood boil. Tell me you don't want me as much as I want you."

She couldn't. "But I don't want to."

Moving his other arm around her, each hand cradling one soft globe, he trapped her gaze in the mirror while he squeezed gently, his body pulsing against her.

"Nor do I, Jillian. But here we are." His hands caressed her with slow, soft strokes, swirling around her breasts, then framing her ribs, the long, dark fingers those of a sculptor, highlighting her form.

She couldn't look away, even as his hands moved to settle on the curve of her hips, squeezing gently. Then they slid to her belly, one hand spreading fingers there as if in possession, the other sliding down to cup her mound.

Jillian gasped but couldn't help rocking into his hand, seeking the caress that tantalized her so. Cullinane smiled, and the effect was dazzling.

She reached behind him and tugged his hair loose from the leather band that held it. Dark locks fell to his shoulders, outlining his dark, compelling beauty, the silver streak at the temple a mark of his power.

"I called you Lucifer," she murmured.

"I'll be your demon lover, Jillian." His silver eyes

glowed, and she fell deeper into his spell. Leaning down, he fastened his lips to her neck, sucking gently. Jillian's head fell back against him and she moaned, her body arching under his hand.

"That's right, sweet one, come to me," he murmured.

Afraid, she fought to remain in control. "No...no, I can't."

"You can, Jillian. You want this, I want this. Just for this moment, forget all the rest."

She shook her head dully, trying to regain her senses, to pull out of the web their desire had woven. "Can't—can't forget."

"Forget what?"

"My—" *My sister,* she'd almost said. Fear shot through her veins, adrenaline surging. Heart pumping, she realized how close to the edge of danger she'd been. Straightening, she stepped away from him, wrapping her arms around her, suddenly naked before him, body and soul.

Oh, God. He'd gotten too close, too near her secrets. She shivered, realizing how much she'd wanted to open up to him, to let down her guard.

Terrified, she stared at him for a heart-pounding moment, chilled to realize how close she'd come to baring her soul to the man who protected her enemy, the man who blocked her goal.

Seeing him standing there, holding her in a gaze so dark and intense—his body ready for her, her own crying out for his even now—Jillian brought shaking fingers to her lips...

Then turned and ran out the door.

Chapter Nine

Cullinane hung up the phone after activating the signal for a meet, his gaze caught by the image on the monitor. The pool glowed azure in the moonlight, and a shadowy figure was moving through the trees nearby.

Jillian. As she approached the water, his gaze scanned her form hungrily, the simple black one-piece swimsuit as erotic as any thong bikini he'd ever seen on the beach. Somehow, just like the woman, what she hid was even more alluring than what she revealed.

He panned the camera in for a close-up, frowning as he took in the lines of strain on her face. The secrets she wouldn't share were taking their toll.

Now her identity wasn't enough. He wanted to know more. Who did she love? Who loved her? Who would send her out and leave her so alone?

Kindred spirits they were, both so solitary, both caught up in lies. In a curious way, she might be his closest counterpart, though she represented his greatest threat.

Somewhere deep, like called to like, and Cullinane wanted to answer.

But even as he watched her arch gracefully into the pool, her arms slicing strong, clean strokes through the water, he knew he couldn't. He didn't dare.

"But someday, Jillian whoever—someday, it's going to be just you and me. Without all that separates us now, we're going to set the sky on fire."

He settled in a chair before the screen, letting his eyes drink their fill of what his body and soul could only crave.

Each stroke through the cool, clear water seemed to drain away some of Jillian's torpor, the deadly lassitude that had held her soul in thrall ever since the morning's shattering encounter in the gym.

She'd spent too much time since then asking herself questions, questions she was afraid to answer. Would Loretta recover if she failed? Was she fooling herself that she could do this? What was it about Cullinane that made her stray from her duty?

She longed for the sweet taste of freedom...of a life no longer bowed down by the obligation to right wrongs that had ended Belinda's life. Hafner's wrongs...her own wrongs... Would she ever again know life out from under the cloud?

She kicked harder, trying to outswim her thoughts.

"The Gulf might be a better challenge. Your space to run seems to be too limited here, my dear."

Jillian flipped to her back at Hafner's words, frowning at the slurring cadence.

"Yes, I'm drinking. I thought you might wish to join me. They say you're not in trouble if you don't like to drink alone." He smiled, waving a bottle of tequila. "Besides, I've got a salt shaker in my pocket and limes right here." He held up the other hand to demonstrate. "Of course—" he chuckled "—that left me no hand for glasses, so we'll have to share the bottle."

"No, thank you."

"No? Please, just one. Then you can sit and talk to me."

It was what she needed to happen, wasn't it? For him to begin to trust her enough to be alone with her?

"All right," she said. "I'm coming out."

Open delight brightened his face. "Good. It's about time." Turning, he moved carefully across the pool deck, headed toward the table and chairs at the end.

Jillian followed, swimming to the steps, then rising from the water, surprised at the chill she felt. Hafner had set his burdens down and returned with her towel, holding it open. When she turned, he wrapped it around her, leaning close. She wrinkled her nose at the smell of his liquor, stepping away quickly.

"Sorry, I forgot. Not in your job description, the watchdog says." With that, he threw back his head and laughed. "Come on, come on." He gestured. "Have a seat."

"The limes aren't sliced," she offered. "Shall I get a knife from the kitchen?"

"No, no." he waved away her objection. "I'm prepared.'' Hafner chuckled. ''Cullinane's no Boy Scout, but I am right now. Be prepared, that's the motto.''

Reaching into his pocket, he withdrew a knife unlike any she'd ever seen. The ornately carved handle carried a design that obscured the necessary button, yet with a whisper of a click it opened, revealing an oddly curved blade.

He saw her study it, and smiled. ''Like it? It was a gift from—a woman I knew.''

She glanced up at his odd tone, studying the faraway look in his eyes. With a slight shake of his head, he turned to her, smiling too brightly.

Jillian's blood chilled. It couldn't be. Shaking off the thought, she watched him cut the limes with the slow precision of a drinker.

Should she ask? Did she want to know?

''Here.'' He held up a section. ''Open your hand.''

Jillian complied, and he placed the lime in it.

''Now curl your hand like this and lick the web between your thumb and forefinger.'' He demonstrated, then poured salt in the wet spot.

Jillian followed suit.

''Now suck the lime, then lick the salt, then take a shot.'' He held the bottle, waiting.

She hissed at the tartness, licked the salt, then took one swig and shuddered.

''There you are.'' Hafner beamed proudly. ''When we hit the bottom of the bottle, I'll let you have the worm.''

Shaking her head, she smiled faintly. ''No more for me, thanks.'' She shivered again. ''I'd better go.''

''Naw, there's a robe in the cabana. Go put it on, then you can use your towel to dry your hair.'' He nodded toward the enclosure. "Pretty red hair, like the glow of the sunset." He nodded sadly. "Pretty red-haired girl." He leaned back heavily. "Go on, Jillian. Or do you want me to get it for you?"

She shook her head, then moved away.

Inside the cabana she found a small closet, first pulling off the towel and wrapping her hair. Then she opened the door and reached inside, unable to see the contents. Her fingers settled on lightweight terry cloth that she drew out, shaking it to be sure no spiders or night creatures had nested within.

When she reached the door, preparing to don the robe, a shaft of pool light slanted through the door and her eyes took in the dark purple fabric, the metallic gold stripe that sparkled in the light.

Belinda. She'd owned a robe like this, one that Jillian had made for her as a joke. They'd had a long-standing joke about Belinda, who adored swimming, being the Queen of the Deep. When Jillian had seen the royal purple fabric, she'd snatched it up. Belinda had laughed when she'd found the inside tag Jillian had embroidered with Queen B.

With shaking fingers Jillian searched the collar, dropping the robe in her haste.

"Jillian? Did you find it?"

"Yes—yes, I'll be right out."

"I'm coming after you," he sang out.

She heard the scrape of his chair and his unsteady step. Cursing the darkness, she stepped outside, hoping to get a quick glimpse of the inside collar band before he noticed.

But he was already there. Snatching it from her fingers, he held it out, like a lady's cloak.

Jillian glanced up at him, slipping it on, her heart gone still and cold. "Whose robe is this?" She held his gaze as if he knew the secrets of the universe.

Hafner shifted uneasily, the life in his gaze flickering out. He glanced away. "Just someone I knew."

She had to know. "A woman?" Turning around, she watched him carefully.

"Yeah." He grew very still, staring off into space. "Someone I—" His gaze dropped to his hands. Staring at them as though they were foreign objects, suddenly he balled them up and stuck them in his pockets.

"Who was she to you?"

Lightning quick, his gaze sharpened, the predator back but not toying with his prey. "Why do you care?" he challenged her, all his bumbling suddenly gone.

Staring into eyes filled with warning, Jillian shivered again.

Hafner stirred, then grasped her shoulders and turned her away, pulling the towel from her hair and beginning to dry it. "She was...no one important." But a slight tremble in his voice said otherwise.

Jillian stood there, letting him rub her hair dry, letting the hands of the man who'd murdered her sister wield a towel gently over her scalp.

The same hands that had held that odd knife, cutting the lime into sections.

She remembered the autopsy report her contact had read to her before the case file had mysteriously gone missing. "Unusual lacerations on subject's body." And Belinda's throat had been slashed.

Jillian jerked away, turning, but Hafner was faster.

Grabbing her upper arms, the light of madness in his eyes, he jerked her against him tightly. ''I'll have you, Jillian,'' he warned, crushing his mouth against hers, stale liquor breath all but gagging her.

She couldn't get room to maneuver; he held her too close. Trying to bring her arms up between them, to move her legs from where he'd locked his around one of hers, trapping her, she jerked her torso back in desperation, tipping their balance—

Then Hafner flew backward, lifted bodily and thrown into the pool, cursing and flailing, spitting water into the air.

Cullinane stepped close, steadying her on her feet. ''Are you all right? I'm sorry. I couldn't get here sooner.''

Jillian stared at him, shaken that Hafner had come so close. ''I should have been able—'' She wondered if he could hear her heart pounding.

''He caught you by surprise, and his hold was too tight. But you would have gotten him off you with a little more time.''

Would she have? Reeling from the shock of the series of revelations, hampered by the tequila, would she have recovered soon enough? And that knife— where had it been while he grabbed her?

''I don't know....'' Again she shivered. Did Hafner suspect? Had she given herself away? Or was he just drunk and making a move?

''Easy, Jillian,'' Cullinane soothed, drawing her close.

Behind him, Hafner bellowed, ''Goddamn it, Cullinane—''

''You're drunk, Klaus. Go to bed before I drown

you myself.'' Voice hard, Cullinane snapped an order to someone she couldn't see. ''Get him out of here.''

Then he tilted her chin up, and his eyes crackled with a tempest of rage and violence and hunger.

Jillian backed away, fighting for breath, shaken less now by Hafner than by Cullinane. She was tired of being strong, tired of holding him at arm's length, tired of fighting herself. The power of the hunger he called from within her frightened her to her soul. She knew she had to keep fighting, but the need of him sapped her waning strength.

''Don't look at me like that,'' she warned, fighting the urge to growl deep in her throat, threatened by the sheer maleness of him, by how closely her hunger matched his.

''Why not, Jillian?'' his low, dangerous voice challenged. ''We've been headed for this since we met.''

''We can't.''

''He can't touch you like that—I won't let him,'' Cullinane raged. Half out of his mind with anger, maddened by longing, he felt the edges of his control unraveling.

He could kill Hafner with his bare hands and not even blink. Thank God Solly had been close on his heels; left alone at the scene, Cullinane couldn't be sure what he would have done. When he'd seen Hafner with her on the monitor, he'd come to attention; when Hafner had glanced at the knife in his hands, he'd come to his feet. When Jillian had entered the cabana in the darkness and Hafner had followed, Cullinane had shot from the room.

But nothing to that point compared with the flash of rage that had run through his body when he'd come through the trees to see Hafner closing in on her, forcing himself upon a woman he had no right to touch. Cullinane had no idea how fast he'd covered the remaining distance, only that the white heat of wrath had seared through his body, wiping out all but the need to make Jillian safe.

Seeing this strong woman scared had been too much. She'd been valiant and resilient through everything he'd thrown at her; the thought of that fierce spirit being diminished by worthless scum like Hafner still had the power to shred his control.

The walls he'd built for so many years buckled under the onslaught of fierce, primal emotion. She was his, and he'd fight anyone who tried to claim her. Cullinane ground his teeth at the image seared into his memory—Jillian at the mercy of Hafner. No matter that she could take care of herself, a desperate desire to erase that image seized him.

It was the match to dry tinder.

Yet even as he reached out for her, he prayed she'd find the strength to stop him.

He didn't think he could stop himself anymore.

"Jillian," he groaned.

Her quick indrawn breath whistled across his lips as he lowered his mouth to hers. Her fingers came between their mouths, her voice breaking the pulsating silence.

"No," she whispered. "We can't…I can't. Don't you see, Cullinane?" she pleaded. She pulled back, voice shaking. "It's just hormones, that's all."

His lips curved sadly. "You know it isn't." It was the worst sort of madness, but in some strange, hurtful way, they'd never had any real choice. "We're alike, you and I, in some way I don't understand. Like calls to like, Jillian. It's time we answered.''

Lowering his head once more to hers, he pulled her close, settling her against him. Cullinane felt Jillian's body arch with longing. He blew a soft, taunting breath over the moisture glistening on her skin. If he could only beat back his craving to bury himself in her, he would walk away.

She'll get you killed, the remnants of his logic pleaded.

I don't care anymore.

''We'll never survive this.'' She echoed his thoughts, whispering against his lips, rising to her tiptoes to pull the leather strip that bound his hair. One arm wrapped around his neck as she slid the fingers of the other hand into his hair. Her nails grazed lightly against his scalp, little shocks of electricity surging through him.

''Forgive me, Jillian. I've damned us both,'' he murmured, his tongue tracing the seam of her lips.

''Then welcome to hell.'' She sighed into his mouth, her tongue already swirling promises too dangerous to deny.

He growled and scooped her up in his arms, covering the distance to the outside door to his quarters without ever breaking the kiss. When they got there, he set her down, fumbling for his keys, trying to still shaking fingers long enough to get inside.

Inside the door at the bottom of the stairs, turning the locks in the darkness, he prayed they would make it to his bed before the fire consumed them.

He wasn't making any bets on it.

He'd hungered for her for a lifetime and never

known it. How he'd ever let her go was beyond him now, a thought burned away by the heat roaring through his veins, melting all resistance, vaporizing all thoughts of anything but the feel of her, the heavy silk of her hair, the satin of her skin, the endless, aching need to be inside her.

Gripping her too hard, he battled to back away, but when he tried, Jillian's nails dug into his shoulders, her lips hungrily seeking his. Electrified by her touch, by the taste of her mouth, Cullinane pulled her hard against him once more.

Jillian moaned, then gasped for air, her body curving back to lie across the stairs, drawing him down against her. He held himself over her with arms gone oddly weak. Those long legs wrapped around his waist as he'd dreamed so often, pressing her mound against him until he thought he'd burst with the pressure building within him.

"Stop, Jillian." He jerked his mouth away. "I need you too much. I won't last if you don't—"

"Now," she gasped. "I want you now."

"No," he insisted, their battles moving to another arena. "We've only got tonight." Needing space to regain his control, he stepped back, dark longings screaming within him.

Jillian's eyes darkened—and then she laughed, a siren's laugh, a woman's dare. Scrambling to her feet like quicksilver, she turned and ran up the stairs in a flash. "Then come and catch me," she challenged. Standing above him, silhouetted in the moonlight slanting through his windows, she slowly dropped the robe to the floor and began to peel off the black suit, one agonizing inch at a time.

Desire of proportions he'd never experienced pounded his conscious mind like waves on the shore, merciless in their roaring, draining him of all rational thought.

Jillian's eyes held his; the challenge in them shot sparks into his belly. If it was a battle she wanted, damn her soul, he would give it to her. With slow, steady steps he climbed toward her, his eyes never leaving the pale skin as the black suit peeled away.

He'd never unleashed the raw depths of himself before, but Jillian had opened the door of the panther's cage and thrown away the key, laughing.

She was magnificent.

Jillian watched his approach with a sudden shiver of delicious fear, her whole body alive and tingling. As he climbed almost within reach, she turned, suit half-off, and ran into the room, the far side of the huge bed her target. She didn't see any of the rest of the room, just the steel gray expanse glowing in moonlight.

Feeling a hand on her shoulder, she whirled, startled, losing her balance and falling backward onto the bed with a gasp. Cullinane stood over her, his smile a white slash against bronzed skin.

She lay there staring at him, mesmerized by the sight of hands reaching down with tantalizing slowness to finish the unveiling she'd started. His long fingers singed her skin where they touched her, his eyes daring her to move, though the clever fingers teased and burned.

With slow grace he slid the garment from her, his gaze sweeping her body, his eyes glowing from within. With one hand, he unbuttoned his shirt slowly, smiling as her gaze followed his fingers, greedy for the sight of more. Stripping off his shirt, he watched her eyes trace the path of the jagged scar on his belly, her fingers rising as if she could soothe remembered pain. For one long, poignant moment, her gaze softened.

Then she smiled, slow and wicked. "More."

He sucked in a breath. "Jillian, you make me crazy." Stripping off the rest in haste, he slid to his knees before her.

Jillian felt the brush of his long dark hair along her thigh send a shock of arousal to tighten her nipples. Her hands curled into fists, crumpling the spread between her fingers. She couldn't stem the quick inhalation that telegraphed his impact upon her.

Head lifting, eyes burning white-hot, his low voice sliding beneath her defenses, he murmured, "I want you crazy, too." Challenge sparked from him as white teeth gleamed from the grin of her darkest longings. He rose to kiss the curve of her hip with exquisite tenderness.

Jillian moaned.

She slid one foot up the inside of his thigh, her instep caressing the curvature of hard muscle, her reward his own indrawn breath.

His smug look disappeared in a smoldering instant.

Her scarlet toenails slid across the straining fullness at his groin. His hands trapped her wrists at her sides.

The clash of wills vibrated in the air.

He's just a man, no one special, she vowed. But Jillian knew she lied to herself. Stiffening to battle the spell he wielded over her, she locked her legs into bands of taut muscle.

His eyes gleamed, strong hands caressing the quivering muscle. Lowering his head to her vulnerable center, his warm breath shot ripples of need through flesh already primed for his touch.

Her muscles softened in shock; her nipples rose; her back arched in pleading. With one soul-shattering stroke of his tongue, he sent her over the edge.

Cullinane drank in the essence of her, feeling her come apart in his arms. He wanted more, wanted to mark her indelibly, make her unable to forget him, no matter what happened later.

Damn her for making him crave this.

He didn't want to, couldn't afford to, was out of his mind to entertain the idea.

But his body didn't care. Surging toward her, every nerve clamored for him to take her. Cullinane descended into the darkness of his hunger, reason smothered in the undertow of forbidden longings, aware only of her thighs softening, her lips slightly parted, her breasts ripe for his mouth to suckle. Whatever reason remained, he ignored. Possessive instincts as old as mankind throbbed through his body, messages he wouldn't deny any longer.

She should be his. He would make her his own, if only for these few hours.

Jillian dissolved his resistance with everything she was, every move she made. The voice that said *Don't do this* was lost in the torrent of his longing.

"Jillian," he whispered. "Let's set the sky on fire." Stretching the length of his body over hers, groaning at the feel of her naked skin along his, he sought her lips once more.

He'd said they were damned, and they would be,

but for now, it was heaven he found in her kiss. Spearing through the darkness of his despair, surfacing in the torrent of need rushing through him, her kiss emerged a cool, clear sweetness that brought moisture stinging to his eyes.

She should be mine.

Maddened by the pain, desperate to possess her, Cullinane rose above her. "Look at me, Jillian," he commanded. Whiskey brown eyes bright with wonder, soft with pain, laced with longing met his gaze.

"Mine," he whispered. "For now you're mine." With one powerful thrust, he entered her body.

Jillian arched toward him as he filled her, swallowing the cry that rose in her throat, her eyes glazing over as ecstasy claimed her. The climax hit her like a wave, sucking her under, drowning her in sensations too powerful to resist. A guttural moan hummed from her throat, a sound so low she felt it vibrating her chest.

Gasping for breath sucked from her body, Jillian scrambled in panic, seeking the surface, but just as she thought she might make it, Cullinane withdrew and her every nerve seemed to follow him.

She sought his eyes, needing reassurance this far outside herself. Naked, vulnerable, stunned by the power of what he could draw from her, she fastened her gaze onto his as if it were the only island in a storm-tossed sea.

He was there, waiting for her, his hunger intense, his eyes challenging her to accompany him. Passion and power crackled and flashed in the heated silver eyes, the sorcerer calling her to step into another realm.

Shivering with nerves, Jillian opened herself more, taking the challenge—stepping to the edge of the world, summoning the courage to leap into a place she'd never been.

Cullinane plunged his fingers into her hair, his eyes flaring with triumph and promise. With the next powerful thrust, he shot them over the edge of the world she knew.

Jillian's head arched back as his mouth sought her throat. She felt herself flying farther with each stroke, her body tumbling through space, Cullinane her only anchor. Streams of sparks shot through the air around them, wind rushed through her hair. But she was frightened no more, exhilaration rushing through her veins like molten gold. Clasping her legs around him, she met every thrust with all the power of the body she'd honed.

Her skin was on fire. Jillian burned up in his magic and welcomed the dying.

Cullinane watched her sleeping in the moonlight, fiery locks spread over his pillow as he'd so often dreamed.

He should have expected her to shake him to his roots, he knew that now. He'd never been out of control like that, never felt such hunger nor such soul-deep satisfaction.

He'd played with fire—and now came the ashes.

He wanted to steal her away to some hidden place, to keep her in his bed until he could slake this thirst for her, which seemed endless.

Which meant, of course, that she was an even greater threat to him than he'd ever imagined. If it were just him, he would keep gambling. He would gladly burn up in Jillian's wildfire, understanding now that he'd never truly lived until she'd warmed his cold, dead soul.

But it wasn't just him; it wasn't even just his ghosts that cried out for rest. It was others, people who had a right to live and love and take a chance at being happy, who would not get that chance if he followed his heart.

His course was set; it had been for a long time.

Even Jillian couldn't change that.

She still had secrets, and he had to solve them. He would sell his soul right now to be able to lock her away safely until this was over, to have a chance to see where this could lead.

But the clock was ticking, and too much was at stake. Drake Morgan's heart didn't matter.

Stroking one lock of her hair, fighting the urge to make love to her just once more, he carefully put distance between them on the big bed, the way he'd have to when morning came. His whole body cried out to hold her, to taste her kisses just once more.

But the clock was ticking, and too much was at stake.

He had no idea how he would deal with her when she awoke. He had no idea what he would find when he dug up her secrets. He could only hope that when this was all over, they would have a chance, that she wouldn't hate him.

Pressing a kiss to the burnished strands, he tenderly laid the lock of hair over her breast, his fingers curling with the need to touch her.

Drawing away, he turned his back to her, settling uneasily on his pillow. Scouring his mind for a miraculous answer, the man known as Cullinane fell into a troubled sleep.

Chapter Ten

The first, faint light of morning awakened Jillian, her body replete with a sense of well-being. For one moment she couldn't figure out where she was. She turned her head and saw the broad, muscled back, the long dark hair.

Cullinane's bed.

Dear God. It all came back in a torrent, remembered sensations swamping her brain. She felt him in every inch of her body, remembered how he'd shattered her mind.

Like calls to like, Jillian, his voice echoed.

But he worked for Hafner, the merchant of death.

Turning to stare at him again, she wished for a moment that she could see his face, could search his gaze for the truth.

Who are you, Cullinane? Why are you here?

And how could a man who protected a murderer have touched her soul the way Cullinane had? How could a man capable of such tenderness ally himself with a vicious animal like Hafner?

Who you surround yourself with is a measure of who you are and who you want to be, he'd told J.T.

Who are you, Cullinane?

Disturbed beyond measure by her thoughts, Jillian arose quietly, slipping from the bed. Padding across the thick charcoal carpet, she scanned the room for her swimsuit, but couldn't see it. She thought he'd stripped it from her somewhere close to the side of the bed where he lay sleeping. Not ready to talk to him yet, she decided to leave it, instead heading for the landing to recover the robe, feeling her cheeks warm as she remembered the challenge with which she'd stripped it off.

She bent to grasp it, and her gaze was caught by an odd glow coming from a room she hadn't noticed last night.

You had eyes for nothing but him last night.

Smiling sadly, she couldn't deny it. Starting to don the robe, she hesitated, then turned the neckline inside out, fingers suddenly trembling.

Queen B.

Oh, God. Jillian shivered, feeling queasy about putting it on, yet needing the contact, however ephemeral, with her sister.

With her duty, her responsibility. The reason she was here.

Lifting her head and drawing a deep breath, she fastened the sash, reminded of what she should not have forgotten in the fire of last night.

Belinda. Loretta. Hafner.

Leave here now, before he awakens and you are forced to deal with what he means to you.

Passing the doorway, she took a quick glance into the room—

And froze in her tracks.

A bank of monitors, like the security room downstairs, but with one major difference. Except for the one screen trained on the pool, all the screens had something in common.

Pictures of her.

With the slow shuffle of a person in shock, she drew closer. Her in the gym...her in the gazebo...her with Alice's children...

Her lying in bed.

A multitude of images caught on tape, images of most of the hours of her day, all on hidden cameras, Jillian under surveillance.

She knew the compound was heavily monitored; her brief tour of the security room downstairs had revealed that the system relied upon surveillance inside and out. Only these rooms and Hafner's seemed exempt.

She'd expected to be caught on cameras at odd times as she went about her duties, but this was different.

This was her bedroom. This was surveillance of *her.* These were not isolated instances, this was Jillian under a microscope.

And this was the man she'd given herself to last night.

She scanned the console, suddenly shaking with fury. He had no right—what else had he taped? In the shower? While she was dressing? Her fingers glided over the controls, confusion scrambling her ability to decipher how to erase these tapes, how to find out what else was on them.

And then a chill shot through her whole body.

Who else had watched her?

And who might have watched them together by the pool last night?

She'd blown it all if Hafner had seen her and Cullinane together. Everything would have gone up in smoke. With the crash of a fist, she hammered at switches blindly, fear of what she'd done making her clumsy.

"It's not what you think." His voice sounded from the door.

Her head shot up, her anger skyrocketing. "Oh, no?" She waved an arm across the bank of screens. "Then just what is˙ this? What else have you watched? Why did you need to strip me last night? You've already seen it all!"

Temper raged through her mind; she could barely hear his words.

"I never watched you naked. It wouldn't have been fair."

"Fair? What do you know of fair? Are there cameras in your rooms?" she raged. "I *sleep* naked," she yelled, pointing at that screen. "You're lying!"

He shook his head, his expression grim. "I only turned on the one in your room after you were asleep. I never—" He glanced away, head shaking again. "It doesn't matter."

"You stripped my body naked last night, Cullinane," she warned, her voice low and angry. "But this—this—'' Her hand swept out, helpless, shaking. ''You've violated my soul.''

''Jillian—'' He started toward her.

Her hand shot out, held up in warning. ''Don't touch me. Don't you ever touch me again,'' she growled. Stabbing a finger back toward the screens, she kept her voice low and deadly. ''Don't ever look in my bedroom again.'' She shoved past him, turning back, her fury surging. ''And if you ever come near me again, I'll kill you, I swear it.''

Shaking with anger, she ran from his room.

Jillian emerged from the shower much later, her skin red from scrubbing, her heart raw and sore. She couldn't shake the memory of the sorrow on his face, couldn't make it square with those pictures on the screen.

Couldn't forget the way he'd taunted, challenged, teased her to heights she'd never dreamed of scaling, shown her glories she'd never imagined.

Held her heart in his hand.

Kissed her soul with an angel's breath.

And watched her when she'd thought herself alone. Stolen pieces of her that anyone could see, moments of her life she hadn't chosen to share.

Watched her asleep, vulnerable and naked…and laid her bare for anyone to watch.

I've got to get out of here before there's nothing left of me. He's already stolen my privacy, my control…my dreams.

I can't let him take my vengeance, too.

She had to find Hafner, had to seduce him, had to get him away, out from under Cullinane's nose. She would gather up what she couldn't bear to leave behind and take it with her, so that once Hafner was dead, she could disappear.

She'd already left behind more than she could spare. Cullinane would have moments of her that she could never retrieve, but he'd have something much more valuable.

He'd have the last shreds of her faith in herself.

She'd come to this place armed with confidence, with cocksure bluster, with a mission to accomplish and the skills to do it. She'd learned hard lessons here, lessons about life throwing you curveballs, about deception and lying silver eyes, about the folly of casting away honor and following your heart.

And now, with faith in herself at its lowest ebb, all she had left was her duty, duty to a dead sister she'd failed to protect.

Somewhere she had to find it within herself to seduce a man she despised, to close off her humanity long enough to snuff out his life with as little concern as he'd shown Belinda.

No one important. That's what Hafner had called her.

Well, she'd been important to Loretta and to Jillian herself. It had taken Jillian too long to realize that loving someone meant loving the whole person. Her contempt for Belinda's choices had isolated Belinda with a man with no conscience, a man who'd found her life inconvenient for his continued success.

Jillian had let Belinda down in the most critical hours of her life. She wouldn't let her down now.

She didn't know how much Hafner would remember of last night; she prayed he didn't know she'd been with Cullinane. But no matter what obstacles she had to overcome, it was time to get this over—and get out.

Dressing with care in a skintight red spandex mini-dress sure to get Hafner's attention, long red dangles at her ears, Jillian left her room.

Now she'd be the predator, in search of her prey.

Cullinane stepped into his shower, sweat stained and weary after his run. It hadn't helped, hadn't erased the memory of her haunted face.

Hafner had only made her afraid.

Cullinane had violated her soul.

It didn't matter that he couldn't explain why he'd kept those tapes, why he'd needed to see her, to try to understand her, to unravel the mystery that was robbing him of sleep. He'd never meant to hurt her, had, in fact, had his own sense of honor about what he would and would not watch.

He had what he wanted, though. The distraction was gone. When he'd watched her in the night, he'd wondered how to achieve the necessary distance to keep from compromising the operation.

He should be happy.

The operation was safe.

But his heart was in shreds.

Memories of Jillian would haunt him forever: gasping in delight, eyes dark with longing. Standing in triumph at the top of the stairs, taunting him with fire in her eyes. Demanding more and crying out when it came.

Coming apart in his arms, flying away with his soul.

He'd never been complete before, but now he knew how it felt. For brief, shining hours he'd touched the purest secrets life had to unfold, known the balm of their blessing, felt the sweetness of a soul mate's kiss, found a home for his weary heart.

But now it was all ashes, the taste bitter on his tongue, and there was nothing he could do to bring her back.

Because duty called. And he had to answer.

He flipped the shower to Cold and hissed at its sting, needing the shock of it to help him gather strength. No need to moon after what he couldn't have forever. He'd been a fool to think he could have it at all.

Thoroughly chilled, he stepped out of the stall, drying off roughly, composing his mind to become detached again. He had plenty to accomplish, first on the list finding Hafner. Walking toward the phone, he avoided the room where he could have checked on his question. He couldn't look at those monitors yet.

"Yes, sir?" Fred answered.

"Where's Hafner now?"

"Getting ready to leave."

"Where's he headed?"

"Just out driving, he said."

"Who's taking the assignment?"

"Jillian, sir."

"Alone?" After last night?

"He said that's all he needed. Want me to ask again?"

"I'll take care of it. Who else is available?"

"Tony, sir, but—"

"But what?"

"Jillian says she doesn't need any help. I asked her if she was sure—you know, after last night and all, but she said they'll do fine. They were laughing about it."

Laughing about it? He shook his head, confused. She'd—

"Sir? You want me to ask her again?"

"No," he snapped. He had to think. "No, just let it go." About to hang up, he jerked the receiver back. "How soon are they leaving?"

"They're loading up the Explorer now, sir. You need to talk to one of them?"

"No, that's all right. I'll be down later." But it wasn't all right; something was wrong. Instincts that had kept him alive for years were rustling. What could she be thinking? Why would she be alone with Hafner?

To hurt me? To get me back? She'd know there could be nothing worse she could do.

But what did he really know about her, about how she thought? Despite the night's magic, she had secrets. She lied every time she answered to a name that wasn't hers. But why would she put herself in close proximity to Hafner when he'd terrified her last night?

It could just be her need to prove to herself that she wasn't afraid; that would be just like her. Afraid of fire? Stick your finger in the flames. Afraid of water? Dive in headfirst.

But he couldn't stand to think of her alone with Hafner, even knowing he had no right to her himself.

Dressing quickly, he strode to the monitors, switching to the camera that panned the garage.

And his heart sank to his toes. What the hell was she doing going with Hafner, dressed like that? Why didn't she just paste a sign on her chest that said Take Me?

Maybe that was what she wanted. Maybe he didn't understand her at all. Maybe moving from his bed to Hafner's was exactly what she intended.

It was a rich revenge, but it would cost her more.

No, he couldn't believe it, not of her. She might lie about who she was, but she was no whore. The woman he'd made love to last night was pure, shining gold, no matter what name she used. He couldn't believe the woman who had yielded to him with such sweetness had it in her to fall into Hafner's arms.

Something was wrong here; something didn't make sense.

Jerking on his shoes with haste, he strapped on his weapon, grabbed his keys and ran down the stairs.

The swamp lay all around them, cypress branches drooping to the water, birds taking flight as they approached. The road was a thin ribbon between marshes.

An alligator waddled across the road ahead. Jillian stopped the car.

"Isn't he a beauty?" Hafner smiled in delight, turning to see her expression. "Ever seen one up close before?"

Jillian shook her head. "He's fascinating, in a horrible way. So ugly he's almost magnificent."

Hafner smiled as if at a bright pupil. "Exactly. There's great beauty in what others see as ugliness. Prettiness is puerile and colorless—it's the strong, the dangerous that I find beautiful." His eyes glowed with that odd light again, scanning her body. "Like you, Jillian. Magnificent. Dangerous and deadly...and magnificent. I can see why you've got Cullinane grinding his teeth."

She stiffened, still not sure he didn't know where she'd spent the night. He was cagey and mean, and it wouldn't be beyond him to toy with her.

"Cullinane's a stone man. His teeth are probably fine."

Hafner chuckled. "Not so stony as you may think."

"What?"

"He's jealous, you know. I think he wants you."

Not anymore. "That's ridiculous. He can't stand me."

He turned a look of pity on her. "Come now, Jillian. Surely you're old enough to know that hate is the other side of love. Cullinane may not *want* to want you, but he does." He chuckled. "He'll hate knowing we were out alone together. But I'm going to love telling him. Oh, yes—turn down this road."

She swallowed hard, caught in his gaze, feeling once again almost as if he could see inside her mind. Pulling her gaze away, she saw that the alligator had slipped into the water, an ally to her plans. Hafner could disappear so easily in these waters, his body never to be seen again.

Jillian started the car, heading toward the clump of trees up ahead and the cabin she could barely see nestled within them.

Nearer, she could see that the cabin was the same weathered cypress as the others they'd passed, standing on stilts, as well. It sat in the middle of a small clearing; at the edges, cypresses grew, small dogwoods scattered here and there. Moss hung low, enhancing the feel of a land that time had forgotten. The light here was umber, the cabin shrouded in shadows, even in the middle of the day.

Hafner got out and closed his door, and Jillian started at the noise.

Don't get spooked. But she couldn't help it. This was where Belinda had died. Her body had been recovered from the waters of this very swamp. The alligators had almost erased the signs of her throat being slit by the man who stood before Jillian now.

His choice to come here was a beautiful symmetry he would never appreciate.

He stepped in front of her where she leaned against the car door. Searching her gaze, he leaned closer, bringing his mouth over hers.

"I'm thirsty." She turned her head slightly away.

Leaning closer, brushing her lips with his, he caressed one breast.

She steeled herself as his lips parted, blanking her mind to endure his kiss.

He stepped away, smiling. "Just wanted a taste of what will come later. Come on inside. Let me get you something cool to drink."

Carefully composing her expression, she looked up and smiled. "I'm ready."

Grabbing their bags from the back, Hafner closed the door and shifted them to his left hand, then took her hand with the other and led her inside.

The interior surprised her, being much less primitive than she would have assumed. Cane furniture was scattered all around on smooth wooden floors, and ceiling fans moved lazily overhead.

"Sorry, no air-conditioning out here," he apologized. "You're welcome to take a shower, if you'd like."

"Not just yet, thanks. I'll take that drink."

"What would you like?"

"Water's fine." She scanned the living room, then followed him to the kitchen, trying to get her bearings.

He turned. "But I brought champagne."

She forced a smile. "Water first." Softening her voice, she glanced up at him with promises. "After we shower, then I'd like champagne."

Hafner's smile turned avid, his eyes hot and hungry. "Water it is." He reached for a glass, filling it with ice cubes, then bottled water, already chilled. After handing it to her, he watched her drink it greedily. When a drop of moisture fell to her throat, he traced it with a finger.

She wanted to run, but she had to stay the course. *Relax, Jillian. No matter what he does, he can't touch who you are inside.*

Cullinane had. But he wasn't Hafner.

But who was he?

When Hafner's hand closed over one breast, she closed her eyes so he wouldn't see her hate.

"Why don't you—" She cleared her throat. "Why don't you shower first?"

His gaze turned greedy. "Why don't you join me?"

She forced herself to meet his eyes steadily, forced herself to smile. "Because—" she traced a finger down his shirtfront "—I need some time...to get things ready."

"Ready?" His eyes lit up.

She smiled. "It's a surprise." Sickness rose in her throat. She couldn't do this.

She had to do it. She'd promised. It hadn't hurt him to snuff out Belinda's life, when she was only an inconvenience, a woman who'd heard the wrong conversations.

How could it hurt her to rid the world of a murderer? It was the only justice Belinda would ever have.

Straightening and forcing another smile, she turned him around and shoved him ahead. "Go on now. Your surprise will be waiting when you get out."

Over his shoulder he shot her a grin that was almost a smirk.

That's the last smirk you ever bestow on anyone, you scum. Hardening her heart, she watched him walk away.

Then she headed toward her purse to get her weapon.

Chapter Eleven

Cullinane slipped inside the door, hearing their voices. He'd been careful to stay far enough back that she hadn't seen him following. What the hell was she doing, coming here with Hafner, dressed in that god-forsaken red dress that would bring a dead man to instant readiness, letting Hafner touch her at will?

He peered around the corner and saw that Hafner was gone. He heard the shower running, then watched Jillian open her purse and draw out her weapon. She moved toward the bathroom and suddenly he knew.

Good God. She was going to kill Hafner.

He closed the distance between them. A chop to the wrist made her drop the gun; at the same moment he clapped a hand over her mouth and dragged her back against him.

Jillian's reactions were instantaneous. One arm

lifted even as she brought her right leg back to destroy his balance.

"Stop it, Jillian. It's me."

She froze, her head jerking around, her gaze meeting his, eyes widening in shock. For one long, tense moment she stared at him, questions tumbling over anger. When she tensed, he pressed his hand more firmly against her mouth.

"Don't make even one tiny move," he warned. Then his own shock surged again, his voice lower, his heart almost pleading for her to deny what he'd seen. "What the hell are you doing?"

Her eyes stared into his, the feel of her body against his sinking deeper into his consciousness. For a moment he thought he'd give anything he possessed to turn back the clock a few minutes—no, several hours.

They stood there, facing the enormity of this discovery. The enormity of all that could never be between them. The horror of what would happen next, once Hafner knew what she was doing there.

Then he heard the bathroom door open and knew they were out of time.

She heard it, too, and stiffened. Gaze defiant, she pulled away from him, and he let her go.

Then Hafner stood in the doorway, towel around his waist. His eyes widened at the sight of Cullinane. "What are you doing here?"

"I might ask you the same, Klaus," he warned, their previous agreement very much on his mind.

He could see Hafner remembered it, too. The pale blue gaze flicked to the gun on the floor, then turned toward Jillian, suspicion creeping over his features.

Then Cullinane did something he thought he might

very well live to regret. Leaning over, he picked up her weapon and handed it to her. In a lazy, chiding tone, he spoke. "Here, Marshall, you dropped this."

Glancing up at Hafner, hearing her quick indrawn breath of surprise, he continued. "She's got good ears—she heard a noise and almost had me."

Tension ran through her frame, still close enough for him to feel it. He couldn't look at her, couldn't even take the time to ask himself why he was doing this, why he was protecting her.

He knew, though. Her life depended upon his convincing Hafner; that had to be his focus. He would deal with Jillian himself later.

Hafner glanced from him to her and back. A panoply of emotions shifted across his features: suspicion, amusement—annoyance at being interrupted in his little tryst.

He turned his attention to Cullinane. "Why are you here?"

"We had an agreement, Klaus." *You fool.*

Hafner stirred uneasily, remembrance of their conversation about not being alone with her until Cullinane agreed clearly running through his mind. "I changed my mind."

"That wasn't our deal."

"So you've reminded me, and now I'm changing the agreement." He was a child, whining at being denied an anticipated treat. Voice turning gruff, he continued, "So you can leave us now and go on back. We're doing fine here."

Jillian's body all but sang with the tension running through her frame, reminding him of nothing so much as a finely tuned piano wire. She still hadn't looked at him.

"Well, there's a problem with that, Klaus, even if I were so inclined."

Hafner had been studying Jillian; his gaze abruptly shifted to Cullinane. "What problem?"

He shrugged. "Something appears to be wrong with my car. I'll need to ride back with you two."

Hafner's eyes narrowed in suspicion. "Call Ron to come get you."

"Oh, I could do that," he agreed, "but then you'll just have more company. And really, Klaus—" He stepped away, needing to get distance from the feel of her. Head nodding toward Jillian, he continued. "Dressed like that, I'm not sure Marshall's prepared to be guarding you all alone out here."

He wasn't sure what he'd expected from her when he'd just saved her neck. But anger was what he was getting—blazing from her eyes. She was furious.

But she was uneasy, too, he could see that. He couldn't blame her—he wasn't quite sure himself why he'd chosen to cover for her. He knew it wasn't just the Bureau's policy of not allowing someone to be hurt just to protect his cover that motivated him.

Whether or not there was ever to be any future for them, there was no way he could turn her over to the mercies of a man with no conscience.

Right now, lust clouded Hafner's normally vicious nature. He'd been on his best behavior since she'd been around because he wanted to bed her.

But it wouldn't last.

Hafner cursed beneath his breath, then all but growled, conceding. "All right, Cullinane. You win."

He turned away, adding in clipped tones, "I'll be dressed in a moment." He left the room.

Relief swamped Cullinane. Then he looked at Jillian's jutting jaw, and fury took over. The raid was only days away, and his life had just become much more complicated.

If he hadn't covered well enough to allay Hafner's suspicions, Hafner could easily get spooked about having her around and change his plans. Years of work could go down the drain—and for what? Who was she working for? Why did she want to kill him?

None of which they could discuss right now.

"Get your things together," he snapped. "Help me load the car." Turning, he headed toward the door.

"Go to hell, Cullinane."

Swiveling his head back to pin her with a stare, he drawled, "I believe we've already been there, Marshall."

The night just past shimmered in the air around them. For a long moment, memories and words that couldn't be spoken trembled in the silence, expectant...tempting...

Forbidden.

Looking at eyes he wanted to tumble into, he turned away instead. "Five minutes, Marshall. We're leaving in the next five minutes."

He held the door open, not about to leave her alone again.

She would have to be watched every minute between now and zero hour.

Jillian drove again, grateful to have something to occupy her thoughts besides the tempest inside her.

Her stomach clenched from anger she couldn't express, confusion she didn't dare ask questions to clear.

Inside the Explorer, silence reigned. Hafner was testy, staring out the window, angry at the change in plans.

And Cullinane just stared at her in the rearview mirror, eyes cold as steel. The forbidding stranger was very much back in place.

Why had he done it? Surely he'd understood where she was headed with the gun; why had he covered for her and not clued in Hafner? He was Hafner's most trusted lieutenant, the man in charge of protecting his life, much too intelligent to miss her intentions. Why didn't he have her bound and in custody now? Why hadn't he explained to Hafner?

It couldn't be sentiment, because right now he looked as if he could gladly choke her himself. Beneath the stone exterior she could see fury simmering.

So when would she pay the price? How would it happen? Could she escape before it did?

And how would she ever get another chance at Hafner?

Her own fury rose in remembrance. Damn him. Why had he followed her? It wasn't just rotten luck— this was a disaster.

All of her plans in ashes, her promises turned into dust. She'd failed, utterly and completely.

The weight of it sank her heart like a stone.

And fear was not far behind. What would he do to her? The waiting was the worst.

Pulling in to the compound, she circled the drive and parked, out of the car in a flash. Her weapon was in her purse; she would abandon her suitcase and hide out in her room until night, then she would figure out some way to leave.

Rounding the hood of the car, she almost made it, but Mary Beth was outside and spotted her.

"Jillian! Can you come see what I made?"

Hearing someone come up behind her, she darted a glance back. Cullinane, grim and intent. Hafner was headed inside.

Picking up her pace, she headed toward Mary Beth and Adam. Alice looked up at her, frowning. Jillian composed her face. Surely he wouldn't do anything in front of the children. If she stayed here with them for a while, maybe she could get away as soon as he went inside. Silently she damned her choice of the red dress. She would stand out like a beacon, trying to slip away.

"Look, I drew a picture of Adam, Jillian, see?" The little girl's excitement contrasted with the impatient look on her brother's face.

Adam glanced up. "Mom, do I have to sit still any longer?" He grimaced.

"Not much longer, sweetheart." Alice searched Jillian's gaze. "Are you all right, Jillian?"

Jillian felt Cullinane walk up beside her. She'd know it was him, if no other way, from the look on Adam's face changing to awe. He, like J.T., worshiped the man.

She wondered if Alice would help her get away.

"Cullinane, look!" Mary Beth held up her drawing. "It's Adam on his skateboard."

She wouldn't have been surprised to hear him growl. He was that angry with her. But to her surprise, he knelt beside the girl, his voice gentle.

"I like it."

Jillian stepped away. "Mary Beth, I have to run now. Alice, would you come inside with—"

His large hand shot out, grabbing her arm. In a silky, dangerous tone, he addressed her. "Oh, I'm sure you have time to look at Mary Beth's drawing. After all, you're not going anywhere...." His gaze was impossible to ignore, but when she glanced down, the cold steel was now white-hot, his jaw flexing. "Are you?"

Alice's gaze narrowed, studying her.

Jillian swallowed. "I guess not." *Stop playing with me, Cullinane. Let's get it over—whatever you intend.*

But he was in no hurry. For several minutes they stayed with the children, the surface conversation convivial and pleasant, the one beneath making Jillian's skin crawl with nerves. Alice kept glancing over at her, but didn't say anything. Finally he excused them both and led her inside with a firm hand locked on her arm.

In the breezeway Ron stopped him to ask questions about his car. Jillian pulled away when he reached into his pocket for his keys. She strode away quickly, then heard his voice behind her.

"Solly, escort Jillian to her quarters." His voice rose a fraction, directed, she knew, at her. "I'll be right there. Wait for me."

She knew an order when she heard one. Searching her memory frantically, she tried to figure out some way to leave right now, but full daylight was hardly a propitious time.

She walked to her room with Solly and, once inside, locked the door, tempted to pull furniture in front of it.

If she did, he would probably bring in a battering ram. Considering his current temper, she decided not to tempt fate. Straightening, she lifted her chin. She was not a child to be afraid of being disciplined. She'd meet him head-on.

Besides, she remembered, he could be watching her right now. She wouldn't give him the satisfaction of cowering. Glancing around the room, she started searching for the camera's location.

Cullinane knew he would have to talk to Hafner soon enough, assess his frame of mind and just how well the gamble had paid off. Walking up the stairs toward Jillian's room, he questioned again what he'd done.

If Hafner hadn't bought his story, not only Jillian but he himself was in danger. As he'd told her before, Hafner truly trusted no one; it had taken Cullinane a long time to work himself into a position where he was as close to trusted as anyone had ever been. But close might not be enough now.

Hafner had made his climb to his current stature on the backs of others. Having killed off foes and friends alike, he was always ready to suspect others of the same intentions.

Cullinane's gamble was risky, but he knew he couldn't do otherwise. The minute Hafner suspected Jillian of trying to kill him, she was dead.

And probably not quickly or mercifully. Hafner had killed no one, at least not directly, since Cullinane had been around. That didn't mean he'd never done it; the Bureau knew he had. He'd just never been caught. Some of the stories were chilling; no matter if Cullinane had hated Jillian, he couldn't condemn her to such a fate.

And he didn't hate her. He didn't have the luxury of exploring his feelings about her now—but he knew they were somewhere on the opposite side of the spectrum from hate.

But she'd lied, and she was still lying. He had to get her to tell him the truth; then he'd decide what to do with her. His options, though, were limited.

Please, Jillian, for your sake—for my sake—for the sake of any future we might ever have had—tell me the truth.

Stopping before her door, he shook his head grimly, then knocked.

No answer. He tried the knob. It was locked.

"Jillian," he warned, his voice low. "Don't jack with me—not now. Open this door."

A long pause ensued. He was reaching for the master key in his pocket when the door opened.

Another time, he would have laughed. Though he never truly knew what to expect from her, in some ways she was utterly predictable.

Redheads and temper. Whiskey eyes spit fire at him.

But the fire barely covered the nerves.

She was afraid, and he wanted nothing more at this moment than to take her in his arms and forget all that was on the line.

So he went on the attack. "Why were you alone with Hafner? Whose idea was it?"

"None of your business." Her glance sliding away, she turned toward the window.

"It is my business, and you know it. What were you doing with your weapon out?" *Talk to me. Tell me it isn't what I think. Help me save you.*

She shrugged her shoulders. "You said it yourself. I heard a noise and was going to investigate. It's my job, after all. I'm a bodyguard."

His own temper shot through the roof. "Damn it, Jillian, stop lying to me." Crossing the few feet between them, he grabbed her arm and whirled her around, grasping her shoulders in his hands, desperate to impress the seriousness of the situation upon her.

Touching her was a mistake. His fingers itched to draw her nearer, his heart worn by the switch from last night's magic to being enemies today.

"Talk to me. I can't help you if I don't know what's going on."

Her gaze remained downcast.

He shook her gently, almost pleading. "I know you're hiding something." *I know you were going after Hafner.* He would give a lot to be able to tell her he, too, wanted Hafner dead, but he didn't dare. She was too much of a wild card.

"Look at me, Jillian." When she refused, he gripped her more tightly, softening his voice. "Please. Talk to me. Make me understand."

Slowly she lifted her gaze to his. His heart pounded with the urgency of his need to know, lifting slightly with the hope that at last she was going to explain. For them to have any hope of a future together, he had to hear the truth from her own lips.

Caught between the powerful draw they shared and

all that conspired to separate them, he felt the poignancy of the moment suffuse the very air around them—shimmering with haunting promise, pierced by stiletto-sharp agony.

And then he knew, could see it in her eyes that she would say nothing, do nothing to save them. All that could have blossomed between them was drowning in a sea of lies.

Cullinane dropped his hands and stepped back, resigned to the knowledge that from here until the end of the operation he would have to be her jailer and she his prisoner. Instead of trying to survive this together, she was driving them further apart.

Heart-weary and drained, he turned away and moved to the door. When he turned the knob, Cullinane stopped, barely resisting the urge to lean against the door in defeat.

"Don't try to run, Jillian. You won't make it."

Without looking at her again, he left.

Jillian couldn't walk the floors any longer, couldn't continue fighting the demons in her mind. Moving to her closet, she selected a change of clothes.

Then she switched off the light, casting the room into darkness, feeling her way back to the pile of clothing. *A little hard to see me in the dark, Cullinane?*

Yet even as she dressed slowly in comfortable dark pants and shirt, she felt a twinge of unease. She didn't like it that he'd had her under surveillance—but she couldn't kid herself about the risk he'd taken for her today.

Why? Why would he do it? Especially after the

way they'd parted this morning. Though he hadn't voiced the words, she was almost certain that he knew exactly what she'd intended, so why hadn't he turned her over to Hafner? What did he have planned for her now?

Was she a prisoner in her room? She'd already decided to test that, to see how far her leash would run. There had to be some way out of the compound. She wouldn't find it, languishing in her room.

Opening the door slowly, Jillian scanned the hall, feeling the comforting weight of her weapon at her back. Cullinane hadn't taken it from her yet, but he'd obviously had a lot on his mind. He would remember it soon; she would have to figure out where to hide it.

But just in case she found a way to leave tonight, she wanted it with her.

No sign of Solly or anyone else. Cursing her unfamiliarity with the monitoring system to which she'd not been given access, she wondered who might be watching her now. Her best avenue was likely to appear to be simply heading to the kitchen for a snack.

The place was very quiet. She wondered where Cullinane was right now. He had the stealth of a panther; she'd better not assume he wasn't somewhere close. He'd certainly done a good job of sneaking up behind her earlier at the fishing camp. She'd never heard a sound.

Traversing the hallway, she passed the library and heard Hafner's voice through the slight crack of the door. Cold and impersonal, his tone belied the words that sent a shiver down her spine.

"—watch on Cullinane. He's behaving oddly. I

don't like it. What?'' He laughed harshly. ''No, it's
not just that he's standing in my way with her.
There's something else going on.'' He cursed vividly.
''If I knew what it was, I'd have already taken care
of it. All I know is my gut tells me to pay attention.
It's what's kept me alive this long.'' Hafner fell silent,
listening.

Jillian could barely breathe, hoping no one would
interrupt and no one saw her on a monitor. But even
so she couldn't leave. She had to hear this.

Hafner sighed. ''You may be right. Perhaps he has
his eye on taking over. It's the problem with capable
men, and Cullinane has certainly been that. But I'm
not ready to retire yet. Nonetheless, I don't like to
think of losing him to an unfortunate accident on the
next operation. He'll be deuced hard to replace. But
he knows too much.''

Jillian's breath caught in her throat. Oh, my God.
Cullinane was in danger. She had to—

Had to what? Warn him? Why? What did she actually know that could help him? And why would he
believe her?

Footsteps sounded in the hall just as Hafner told
his listener goodbye.

Taking quick steps away, then slowing her pace to
make it appear casual, she turned the corner. Alice
was coming her way. She stopped, gaze scanning Jillian's attire as if wondering where she was headed.

Jillian smiled casually. ''Just headed for a snack.''

Alice put one hand on her arm. ''What's wrong,
Jillian? What happened today?''

''Nothing.'' She couldn't involve this woman. Alice had enough on her mind. Peering closer, she realized Alice had been crying. "Are you all right?"

Alice sniffed, pulling at the tissue in her hand. "I wish I had it together like you."

Together? Jillian stifled the urge to laugh. She squeezed Alice's shoulder. "I have no idea how you juggle all you do, Alice." Right now, all she wanted to do was run—run away from this place, run toward Cullinane.

"I wish I had the nerve to leave here. But I can't."

"Why not?"

"I owe it to Klaus. He's done so much for me. And I could never support the kids on what I could make."

"You're miserable here, Alice."

"I can't put what I want ahead of what they need. I have to be strong enough to stay and take control. You could do that, Jillian—I wish I were as sure of myself as you are."

Sure of herself? What a laugh. For one instant Jillian wanted to confide in someone. In an odd way, she and Alice faced the same dilemma. What was the right thing to do for those you love? How much of yourself did you give up to do it?

Play it cool, Jillian. You don't have that luxury. You've got a more immediate problem—you've got to regain some of your foothold. Without the ability to move around, she would never be able to get close to Hafner—or to get out.

Jillian pasted on a smile and listened to Alice pour out her troubles. But she listened with only half an ear. Around and around, the questions spun in her brain.

Was Cullinane in danger? And was it her fault?

Chapter Twelve

Late that night, Cullinane returned to his rooms after calling Alonzo from a pay phone inside a bar. He hadn't been tailed, but that was the only good news from this very long day. As was his daily habit, he swept the rooms to assure no bugs had been planted while he was out.

Now he knew who she was, but knowing only made his job harder. A former cop, for God's sake—he had to thank Alonzo's guys. Someone had had the foresight, when her prints came up with no match in their computer, to send them out to law enforcement agencies across the country, thinking that her skills might point to a background as a cop.

Bingo. Her name really was Jillian, and he couldn't help feeling a sense of relief that in his private thoughts he wouldn't have to change. She'd been smart, though—Marshall was her mother's maiden name. A tough connection to make on the computer, unless you knew what you were looking for. Simple for her to remember, but hard for them to trace with no other identification.

Jillian Blake, that was her real name. Jillian Marianna Blake.

Stepsister to Belinda Blake, Hafner's murdered mistress.

So now he knew. Now he understood. Now he even sympathized.

But it only made things worse.

As he stepped toward the window, his thoughts matched the unsettled weather outside. Remnants of a hurricane boiled up from the coast, turning the night as restless and angry as Cullinane himself felt. For the first time since entering, he really looked at the room he'd left so hastily this morning. A scrap of black peeked from beneath the rumpled bedspread. He recognized Jillian's black swimsuit, and his heart twisted as memories swamped him.

Had it been only last night that they'd loved so explosively? Touched souls with such tender grace? The memories seemed years ago, yet he'd never forget a single one. He would be haunted by Jillian to the end of his life, but now his chances of anything else with her seemed more remote than ever.

He understood now why she'd lied to him at every step, marveled at the courage she'd demonstrated in showing up at the compound, in tackling this alone, no backup at all.

He understood, and might even have done the same himself. His respect for her had only increased. But it didn't matter; he didn't—couldn't—trust her. He now knew she was more dangerous than ever.

Because this was personal. She wasn't just a hired killer. Jillian was bent on revenge for her sister's murder. She was skilled and dangerous—and obsessed. She'd shown a nerve and valor any man he'd ever known would be hard-pressed to match. But that nerve sprang from obsession, from a single-minded goal that put his own in peril.

He wished he could talk to her, explain that he understood, but that would lead to inevitable questions from her about why he sympathized when he was Hafner's right-hand man. Maybe if she'd come clean with him of her own free will, he could consider telling her a little, asking her to join him.

It wasn't that he didn't understand why she would hold back, thinking about his involvement what she surely must. But he'd taken a huge risk for her, and she had to be aware of that. He'd gone past sense and begged her to tell him the truth so he could help her. Those actions gave her a signal that she had to answer.

But the actions were as far as he could go for now. Until and unless she took the next step and gave him her truth without being forced, he could never give her his own. And without her truth, he had no choice but to keep her under constant watch, now more than ever. It would simplify his life if he could send her away and keep her from interfering until this operation was over in a few days. But he doubted now, after what he'd learned, after seeing Jillian's determination in action, that she'd ever give up trying to kill Hafner, unless she was dead first.

He couldn't let that happen, nor could he let her take Hafner down. Not this close to the end. His only choice was to keep up his juggling act with Hafner and keep Jillian near.

And hope to God he could keep her safe.

Never had he wanted more to catch a glimpse of her, if only on the monitors—but he could still remember the devastated look on her face when she'd seen the bank of screens. Though his looking had had to do only with longing and not surveillance, he couldn't betray her by looking now, though she would never know.

He would watch her again, but only to guard her. But for tonight, he would leave her in peace.

Jillian waited until long after the household was asleep, the hallways silent and dark.

Then she crept down to the library to use what she suspected to be an unmonitored phone line. So far at sea, so much out of her element, she needed to talk to someone friendly, to try to get her bearings.

It would still be far too late in San Diego, but she had to try. Perhaps Hiroshi's calm guidance would steady her as so often before.

"Yes?" His voice, so quiet and still, sounded wonderful.

"Hiroshi," she began, "I'm sorry it's so late. I—I had no choice."

"What is wrong, Jillian? Why do you call? Are you in trouble?"

Yes. Oh, yes, but it's trouble of my own making.
"No, I was just worried about Loretta. How is she?"

"Loretta is not well. You should come back. She worries. It has been too long that you are gone."

"But my promise—I must keep it."

"Promises, kept or not kept, will do her not so much good as to see you, to have you near. Come home, Jillian, and cease this quest for vengeance."

"I— Even if I could live with myself for giving up, I can't—" She stopped, thinking she heard a noise in the hall.

"You are there, Jillian? You are in need?"

No more sounds, but she didn't dare take a chance on anyone tracing Loretta or Hiroshi. "I have to go now, *sensei*. Please—tell Loretta I love her and I will be back soon." *Please, God, let it be true.*

"Jillian, you are strong enough to meet any challenge, but I ask you this one thing—what will this quest of yours cost your soul?" He'd never approved of her plan or her methods; it was a sign of his concern that he still watched over Loretta for her while she was gone. "Come home, Jillian. Bury your vengeance. Let your sister's soul rest."

"Belinda won't rest until I do this, *sensei*. Nor will Loretta." *Nor will I.* Heavy of heart, she told him goodbye, then sat in the darkness, wondering what to do. The gathering storm outside howled out her turmoil.

If she warned Cullinane, would he believe her, already knowing she'd lied? And if he did believe her, what would he do? Would he leave to save himself?

She was almost certain the answer to that was no. So what would be gained?

Would she cancel her debt to him for this day's

rescue if she told him? Would he back off on the watchdogs, giving her a chance at Hafner again?

Not hardly.

Most likely he'd watch Hafner even more closely, and she'd never get another chance at the man.

Sitting back heavily in the chair, Jillian wavered, for the first time, on a goal that had driven her for many, many months. Was Hiroshi right? Should she find some way to convince Cullinane to let her leave and go home?

Belinda was dead. Her stepmother needed her.

Would she add to the mounting cost the life of a good man?

A good man. A man who did not deserve to die at the hands of an animal like Hafner. Images she'd fought to forget rose up to haunt her, images of the night passed in Cullinane's arms. Whatever the reason for those pictures of her on the bank of monitors, she hadn't let him explain, too caught up in her fixation on Klaus Hafner, too quick to leap to assumptions.

But over and over, however stony he'd been, she realized now how often Cullinane's actions had been at odds with his image. He talked tough, he was tough, but beneath was a good, decent man. A man who cared about a young boy going astray, who would take time for a little girl's pictures. A man who'd taken her to heights of glory with a power and tenderness that still made her shiver.

Though she still didn't know why he was with Hafner, she did know he'd put himself at risk for her more than once.

How could she do any less? Would Belinda rest

easier, Loretta find peace, if a good man died while Jillian stayed fixed on vengeance?

Her weary heart gave the answer. He might not believe her, might think she just wanted to cause trouble between him and Hafner—it might all blow up in her face and cost her the chance to avenge her sister.

But to live with herself, Jillian had to try.

Rising from the chair, she made her way quietly upstairs. Outside his door she paused, wondering if she should wait until morning. Before she could lose her nerve, she knocked.

"Who is it?" He didn't sound sleepy, despite the late hour.

"It's me, Jillian. Please—could we talk?"

The door jerked open, a faint golden light coming from the table by the bed. The silver streak at his temple seemed to glow; his eyes were wary and remote. He wore only a pair of sweatpants, his broad chest seeming to fill the doorway. Her gaze fell inevitably to the jagged scar bisecting his flat belly, a vivid reminder that he'd been harmed before—and could be again.

Lifting her gaze once again to his, she curled her fingers into fists to keep from touching him. "There's something I need to tell you."

A spark leapt in his gaze, quickly shuttered. His low voice rumbled inside that muscled chest. "Come in," he said, carefully neutral. Stepping aside, he closed the door quietly behind her.

Once she was inside, her gaze lit upon the bed, rumpled now as it had been when she'd left it. The press of memories choked her with their aching sweetness, her mind awash with longings. She could feel him at her back, tense and waiting, but stared instead at the rain driving against the windows, hearing the angry howl of the wind.

He had to believe her, no matter what he chose to do. Suddenly she couldn't bear it if anything happened to this man with whom she'd shared so much. Theirs might be a strange intimacy formed of battles and lies, but at the base of them, she thought she agreed with him.

Like called to like.

Jillian turned around, hoping for the right words to convince him. Straightening her shoulders, she met his gaze.

And saw pain, quickly masked. He remembered, too.

Swallowing heavily, she began, barely able to keep from looking at the floor. "I know I haven't, that is, I—I need you to believe me, even though you think I'm a liar." Drawing a deep breath for courage, she hurried on. "You took a big chance for me today. I think you're in danger now, and I want to help you."

Cullinane shook his head to clear it, her words not at all what he'd expected to hear. "What are you saying?"

She stared at him intently. "Tonight I was on my way to the kitchen when I heard Hafner in the library. Is that phone line monitored?"

He frowned, wondering why she asked. "No."

For a moment an odd expression flickered over her face, something like relief.

"Go on," he urged.

"He was— I don't know who he was talking to, but—" Her gaze seemed almost desperate. "I don't think he trusts you anymore. I think he's planning for something to happen to you soon. He mentioned an operation.''

Oh, God. That was all he needed, for Hafner's antennae to go on full alert. But what did he expect after the gamble he'd taken?

"Tell me every word."

Her eyes cleared. "You believe me? I—I was afraid that after…''

He knew exactly what she meant, but couldn't afford to discuss it now. Curtly, he nodded, frowning. "I need to hear exactly what he said."

Jillian closed her eyes briefly, then recited. "He said something about keeping a watch on you, that you were behaving oddly. Then the other person must have said something about—'' She glanced at him, color staining her cheeks. "About me, because Hafner said it wasn't only because you were—'' Her color deepened, and she cleared her throat. "You were standing in the way with me.'' Voice firming, she continued, "He said that he just had an odd feeling and that he trusted his instincts after all these years.

"Then he said that maybe it was just that you wanted to take over his operation, that it was what happened when one hired capable men. He said that—'' Jillian reached out and grabbed his arm, the feel of her jolting him, her eyes going dark and intense. "He said that he'd hate to have an unfortunate accident happen to you on the next operation but that you knew too much.''

Squeezing his arm more tightly, she stepped one step closer, her voice soft and low. "It's because of what you did for me today, isn't it? Because you covered for me. Now you're in danger because I—'' Ingrained caution stopped her. "You have to believe me, Cullinane. You have to get away, before it's too late."

"Will you go with me?" He was curious now.

She looked away, dropping her hand. "I can't."

"Why not, Jillian? What's keeping you here?" *Please tell me, please give me the truth.*

Jillian paced, nearing his window and staring outside at the lashing rain. He wanted to go to her, to drag the truth from her, but it meant nothing unless she gave it to him of her own will.

For endless moments he stood there waiting, watching the tension in her frame, knowing that he needed her help, her cooperation—but only if he could trust her. And the beginnings of that trust would be found in tearing down the wall of lies between them. She had to take the next step.

With the courage he'd always admired in her, Jillian straightened and turned to face him, tossing her fiery locks as if to defy the unsteady nerves he could see in her eyes.

"My name isn't Marshall. It's Jillian Blake. I came here to kill Hafner because he murdered my sister and walked away scot-free."

Cullinane closed his eyes in thanksgiving, then hastily opened them, willing her to continue. She stared at him intently, as if wondering what to say next.

"Did you know her? Belinda Blake?"

He shook his head. "I've heard her name, but she was—gone—before I came."

Eyes unutterably sad, she continued. "Belinda was

my stepsister, really, but we were closer than blood. Her mother, Loretta, is the only real mother I've ever known. She was always wonderful to me, treating me like I was her own." When she glanced up, the pain in her gaze made him ache with the urge to go to her. "That's why it's so hard to live with knowing that Belinda's death is my fault."

"How can it be your fault?" He sensed he was hearing the truth behind her single-mindedness, the pain that pushed her to such an extreme risk.

"She—I just thought she was being rebellious, just too hardheaded to admit she was wrong. I turned my back on her when I found out she was the mistress of a criminal and she was using drugs pretty heavily." Glancing up, her eyes showing no mercy to herself, she continued. "I was a cop, you see, and I couldn't understand why she wouldn't get her act together, why she kept causing Loretta so much pain. Belinda was—she always took the easy way out, always expected me to cover for her. I mean, I loved her, but time after time I'd bailed her out and tried not to let Loretta know what trouble she'd made. But finally I decided—"

Jillian's voice broke, and then he didn't resist any longer. Crossing the room, he pulled her into his arms, but she shrugged away, stepping back, one hand held up.

"No," she said firmly, shaking her head. "I don't deserve—I can't accept comfort. Not after what I did."

But her eyes said she wanted it in the worst way. Standing close, ready to help her whenever she'd allow, he merely nodded. "All right. So what happened next?"

Jillian's eyes flashed with anger and regret. "What happened next was that I decided it was time for tough love. I cut Belinda off, refusing to take her calls or talk to her after delivering an ultimatum that she leave this man she was living with in New Orleans and enter a rehab program." Glancing up with eyes so raw they hurt his own heart, she continued. "I told her I wasn't bailing her out again, that I didn't want to hear from her until she was calling from a clinic."

Her voice dropped to a whisper. "I never heard from her again."

"Jillian, you can't—" He reached out, wanting to ease her.

She held up a hand and stepped backward. "No, wait. There's more."

Glancing out the window, she continued. "After we received the call from the parish sheriff's office when her body had been found, I tapped some of my connections to see what could be done to expedite the case."

The Jillian he'd first met stared at him now, her body straight and tense with defiance. "It didn't take me too long to find out that they knew who it was who'd done it—and had no intention of making the arrest."

Cullinane winced, knowing that his deep-cover operation had been under way by then. With no evidence to prosecute Hafner, the decision had been made to press forward to nail him in the much bigger arena of arms dealing and terrorism. He'd never heard, though, about a sister—or her investigation.

Jillian looked up at him, her wounded heart in her eyes. ''I wanted to come here, but I needed my job to take care of Loretta. I tried to push them from California. For a long time I kept Loretta's hope alive that justice would be served, but finally she couldn't stand any more. In total despair, Loretta tried to commit suicide, and almost succeeded.''

Good Lord. And Jillian had taken everything on her slender shoulders.

Drawing a deep, shuddering breath, she pushed onward, her eyes dark and penetrating, willing him to understand. ''I had to do something, find some way to make it right, to give Loretta a reason to live again, to put Belinda's soul at peace.'' Her voice dropped to a whisper. ''To forgive myself.'' Lost in thought, she stared at the floor.

Her pain undid him, her wounded soul speaking out to his own. He had to give her hope, make her see she wasn't alone. Moved by the gift of her truth, he decided to share his own. They were on the same side, after all; his relief was boundless.

''Jillian.'' He put his hope into the speaking of her name. ''Hafner will pay for what he's done. I'm going to make sure of it.''

Her head rose swiftly, shocked surprise in her gaze. With a frown of incomprehension, she shook her head. ''Because he's after you now?''

''Because he's an animal, a vicious killer who's been responsible for the deaths of hundreds, maybe thousands, all over the world.'' Grasping her by the shoulders, he felt happiness surge within him that he could offer her this. They didn't have to battle anymore. He would help make things right for her, and for her sister.

"I'm going to take him down, Jillian. I'm not what you think. We're on the same side. I'm an FBI agent. I've been undercover on this case for two years. You don't have to do this by yourself anymore. Leave Hafner to me—I promise you he's going to pay, and soon."

Jillian stood stock-still, her eyes going wide. His heart still swelling with relief and optimism, he was unprepared for her violent reaction.

"No!" Jerking away from his hands, she backed up, shaking her head rapidly, burnished hair swinging wildly in denial.

He frowned, confused. "Do you understand what I'm saying? We're not at odds. I want him, too. I've spent years of my life going after him. You're not alone anymore, Jillian. We're going to take him down along with his whole network, then he'll never harm anyone again."

Her eyes sparked fire, and she still shook her head. "He won't—he'll get away this time, too."

"No, he won't. I'll make sure of that."

Her eyes sought his in pity, as if he were the one who didn't understand. "I can't trust that."

He was surprised how much it hurt. Voice turning softer, he sought to persuade. "I promise you that you can."

"I'm sure you mean that, but I've seen what happens. I've been in the system, remember? I know how often it fails."

Clenching his jaw, he pushed back his anger. "You

haven't seen me. You don't know how much I want him.''

Jillian's eyes softened slightly. "I'm sure you do, but you know yourself what happens when lawyers and juries get involved. We've all seen the bad guys walk away a thousand times.'' Her own voice hardened. ''And I've been promised justice for my sister's murder before. It didn't happen.'' Gaze almost pleading, she urged him to understand. ''I can't take the chance again, Cullinane. Loretta won't ever get better if he walks away again. I'll lose her—and I'll have no one.''

You could have me. Warring impulses tore at him. He wanted to go to her, to pull her close and soothe her until she relented. But anger simmered that she could doubt him. It didn't matter what the system had done before. Hafner *would* pay, damn it. He couldn't live with anything else. Grasping for patience, he tried again.

''It will be different this time, I promise. Nothing short of dying will stop me from taking him down.''

Her gaze sparked. ''You're going to kill him?''

Cullinane shook his head. ''Not if I can help it. I want his whole network, all his terrorist buddies, all his contacts. I want to wipe his influence off the face of the earth.''

He could feel her withdrawing, the icy facade forming again. ''He has to die. Can you promise me that?''

''I'm an officer of the law, Jillian, not a vigilante.'' When her eyes went dark with pain, he almost stopped. ''You've been a cop—you know I can't kill him in cold blood, no matter how much I hate him.

But he will be punished. Have faith in me, if not the system.''

He pressed the point. "Have you ever killed anyone before, Jillian?"

"Once."

"How far away were you?"

She'd been across the street; it was a sniper shot. She shook her head. It didn't matter. She had to do this.

"Talk to me."

"Talk won't help. He has to be punished. I can't sleep. All I do is dream about her, about Loretta. He has to die."

"But not at your hands. He *will* be punished. I promise you that. But if you kill him in cold blood, you're no better than he is."

Jillian saw Cullinane's jaw flex, saw the plea in his gaze as he concentrated on her.

Hiroshi's voice echoed in her mind; she thought of his disapproval, his plea for her to forget about vengeance. She was tired, so tired. She just wanted this over.

"This isn't who you are, Jillian. You were a cop. You took an oath."

"I'm not a cop now."

"But you're still that same person inside. The only one who's going to pay, day after day, will be you. Hafner won't feel a thing."

"But he'll be dead. Belinda will leave me alone. Loretta will feel better."

"You think Belinda would want you turning into an animal, no better than Hafner? Is that the sister she admired? And is Loretta really going to be happy to welcome a murderer back? She needs your strength, not your vengeance. You don't need to earn Belinda's forgiveness. You only need to earn your own.''

Jillian tried to picture taking the shot, the gush of blood—

Her stomach roiled at the thought. Was he right? Was that why every time she'd been near Hafner, she'd held back? Because she was weak?

"I'm not a coward," she declared, glancing at Cullinane.

"No, you're not. It took guts to come into a place like this alone. But I'm begging you, Jillian—for your own sake, for the sake of what's between us, please trust me to take care of this."

She felt dizzy, grasping for a foothold in the disordered landscape of her thoughts.

Cullinane seemed to sense it. He pushed harder. "There's something strong between us, but love can't thrive in a climate of hate. You're not a hater by nature. Please don't do this to yourself, don't damage your soul."

Watching the battle go on within her, he could only wait and pray he would win. For endless moments she gazed sightlessly at the storm, her distress feeding his own. He had to win this battle; the stakes had never been higher. Not only his operation but their future was on the line. His own newborn faith in her had been shaken when she hadn't believed him; no matter how much he wanted her, how much his heart cried out to hers, he could not throw away years of pain and effort.

Failing to stop Hafner once had haunted him for years. Dead children cried out for justice. Cullinane understood exactly how she felt, but too much was at stake now. Too many lives were involved.

Even if they weren't, he couldn't let her do this to herself. She wasn't a cold-blooded murderer.

When she turned back to face him, his heart sank like a stone. Written quite plainly on her face was her refusal; the sorrow filling her eyes gave him no comfort.

Desperate to change her mind before words sealed their fate, he moved to her, drawing her close. "Don't do this to us, Jillian. What we had here last night..." He didn't have the words.

Words were the enemy. Somehow he had to convince her not to doom them both. Pulling her close, sliding the fingers of one hand through the fiery silken hair, he brought his mouth close to hers, hearing her soft sob of anguish.

Bittersweet desperation colored his kiss. When her mouth softened beneath his, his heart surged with hope. She had to understand, had to work with him. She couldn't do this, couldn't condemn them to the loneliness again. Not now, not when he'd just found her. Not when there was a path to the sunlight, if only she would believe.

He felt her aching, her longing for him. For a sweet moment in time, he was thrown back into the bliss, the night of magic they'd shared. Jillian reached out to him, pressing herself close.

For a moment he dared to believe they would win.

But all too quickly, he felt her draw away. With infinite sadness, her lips told their fate. When she pulled back, he didn't try to stop her, hard knowledge settling painfully in his chest.

"I'm sorry," she said softly, her voice shaky but resolute. Lifting her gaze to his, her eyes haunted, she spoke the words that would damn them. "I'm sorry— I can't take the chance."

Chapter Thirteen

Jillian watched him struggle, the mask coming with more difficulty than before. Feature by feature, his face hardened into the forbidding man she'd first met.

The eyes hurt her most, for there the man who tortured her dreams still lived. His voice low and aching, he spoke. "You know I can't let you try again." Intently, he pressed on. "Lives depend upon it, Jillian, not just mine. I can't let you compromise the plans under way."

Voice turning steely, he stepped closer. "Give me your weapon." He held out his hand. "I don't want to have to arrest you, but I will if you force me to it. I want your promise that you won't interfere. I need a week."

"You don't have any grounds to arrest me." She backed away, her pistol still at her back.

He followed. "Oh, but I do. You're interfering with a federal investigation. I only need to buy time, and I'd get that with you in jail."

"I don't think you'd do that. You can't arrest me— unless I go quietly, you'll blow your cover."

Hard and implacable, steel gray eyes speared her. "You wouldn't be here now if you were prepared to sign my death warrant."

Jillian searched frantically for alternatives, knowing she couldn't run. She was fast, but he would have her before she reached the door. And even if she made it past him, she'd never make it out of the compound.

She was a good fighter, but he was better.

And he was right about what had brought her to this room. She'd come to save the life of a good, decent man—more decent, even, than she'd known then. He was one of the good guys. God knows what it must have been like to be undercover with Hafner for two long years.

Whatever her reluctance to trust the system with Hafner's demise, she couldn't stand by and watch him murder Cullinane. She would never forgive herself.

Perhaps if she agreed to cooperate, she would have a chance to do both: watch Cullinane's back and take care of Hafner. But as things stood now, she could do neither. If she boxed Cullinane in a corner, she had no doubt he would do what he said. She would be locked away, no weapon at hand, helpless to do anything. Free, she had a chance to do both.

Stalling for time, she retorted, "Who's going to watch your back with Hafner? All the men are his."

Maybe this would work; she had to convince him. "You need me to watch your back. Hafner's going to try something and you're alone inside here, aren't you? You have no one to trust, either.''

He didn't respond, merely watched her with wary eyes.

Holding her hands up in surrender, she drew herself up and met his gaze. ''Let's make a deal.''

Cullinane went very still. ''What do you mean?''

''I still don't trust the system, but I'll give you your week. Once it's over, I won't make any promises. If you don't get him, I have to go after him. But for one week, you need my help.''

''Why should I believe you? You've made it very clear that you don't think I can handle him.''

''I didn't mean that.'' Exhaling in frustration, she strove for calm. ''It's not you I don't trust. I believe you'll try to see that he's punished—I just don't believe you'll succeed. A guy like Hafner has spread money everywhere. Who knows what cops he's bought, what judges he's got in his pocket? If he's operating on an international scale, he could have people in Washington on his side, for all you know.''

Seeing him about to protest, she held up a hand. ''But it doesn't matter what I believe or you believe, the fact remains that Hafner's suspicious of you and is planning to get rid of you. Whatever the forces you may be able to tap outside—in here, I'm the only person you can count on.''

''Why? Why would you do it?''

Why should you believe me, you mean? I'm not sure you should. She didn't know what she would do, if push came to shove, if she got a chance at Hafner. But she also knew she couldn't let Cullinane die.

''You can remember last night and ask me that?''

she demanded. "No matter how much stands between us, Cullinane, I'll remember last night for the rest of my life." Her voice growing husky, she swallowed hard. "I won't let that murderer have a chance to kill you, too. No matter what else you think, believe that. I'll watch your back."

"And if you get a chance at Hafner?"

He saw her too well. Jillian shook her head. "I can't promise you that I won't take it, but I won't seek it out."

"Jillian, I can't—" Swearing darkly, he ran impatient fingers through his hair.

"You need me, Cullinane. Take what I can give you."

He studied her carefully. Could he trust her? Or the war inside her heart? On some levels, he thought he could; any woman who would go to the extremes she had for love of her family had loyalty in abundance. For those she cared about, she would go to the wall.

But where did he fit into all that? Yes, he remembered the night before in riveting detail. He, too, would never forget it. In the hours they'd come together, battles set aside, he'd been shaken to his foundation by how deeply he'd felt about her. There had been magic, and it might just be enough to get them through.

But her loyalty to her family, the guilt she wouldn't shed—those, too, pulled at her. Fierce in her hatred, she was also fierce in her love. This dilemma would put her to the test.

She was a strong woman and unlike anyone he'd ever met. In another life, he would have stopped at nothing to make her his.

But he didn't have that luxury now. Yet what choice did he have? If he dispatched her from the compound, Hafner's instincts would overload. His own situation was too precarious; everything depended on quieting Hafner's instincts. That meant business as usual, for four more days.

He'd told Jillian a week, but the actual date was four days away. If he could keep her close at hand, guarding his back, he could also prevent her from having a chance at Hafner. If he kept her in the dark about details of the raid until the last minute, she couldn't plan to subvert them.

Cullinane didn't see what choice he had. He would have to alert Alonzo and the others to help him watch her once the raid was under way, but in the meantime, he would have to watch Jillian as closely as he watched Hafner.

He didn't doubt she would protect his back. But he also didn't take her warning lightly. If she got a chance at Hafner first, Hafner was dead. It might not be the end of the world, since elements of the network in Italy and Germany would be rounded up simultaneously with the raid in New Orleans. But he had no way to be sure what signals Hafner might be sending out; his lack of response before the raid might alert someone and ruin it all.

He had to keep Hafner alive. If it took watching Jillian every second, then that's what he'd do.

"All right." He held out his hand. "But I want your word."

Slowly she reached out toward him. "How do you know my word's worth anything?"

Clasping her smaller hand tightly, admiring the

strength it must have taken to face him down, he smiled. "I don't, not for sure. But isn't that what trust is about, Jillian?"

A flash of pain in her eyes told him he'd scored a direct hit.

Jillian stood on the driveway shooting baskets, trying to pass the time that seemed endless, the waiting game that stretched her nerves to breaking. If Cullinane wasn't watching her every minute, someone else was. Today it was Tony.

Suddenly she noticed Tony straightening. Jillian turned, expecting to see Cullinane behind.

But it was Hafner. J.T. fell silent.

"I don't want to interrupt your game." But his eyes said differently.

J.T. retrieved the ball. "I've got homework, anyway." Nodding at her, he moved away. "Check you later."

"Sure," she answered, not liking the way Hafner's gaze swept over the sweat-soaked shirt clinging to her skin. "What's up?"

"I merely wanted to see how you were getting along. We haven't had a chance to speak since our little jaunt."

What did he want? Why was he bringing it up now, three days later? And how did it play with his plans for Cullinane?

Placing one arm across her shoulders, he led her inside. "Let's have a drink, shall we?"

Jillian fought the urge to shrug off his arm. Tony followed them at a discreet distance. What had Cullinane told Hafner since that day? She'd seen them together several times, conversing intently. How could she cover for Cullinane when she had no idea what he'd said?

He himself had kept her at a distance. Often nearby, he'd made sure they were never alone. Yet she'd caught him several times, gazing at her intently, curiously...sometimes longingly.

The war of nerves was getting to her. She wanted this week over in the worst way.

Hafner led her up the stairs and into his quarters, rooms she'd never seen. He nodded at Tony to close the door. She couldn't help wondering if these rooms were monitored. Cullinane's weren't; she wondered if he dared watch Hafner, and if so, how he could hide it. Jillian marveled afresh that Cullinane had kept his subterfuge going for two years. The man must have nerves of steel.

She'd been doing it only a week, and she was exhausted.

Glancing around the room, dark though daylight was bright outside, she looked for clues to understand Hafner, to understand what Belinda could have seen in him.

Black and gold, mostly black. Everywhere. His bed was draped at the corners with gold-on-black patterned silk, hanging from the ceiling. It resembled bed hangings she'd read about in medieval romances.

The walls were a dark charcoal, wooden floors teak, scattered with rugs she supposed were expensive; she'd certainly never seen any like them before.

"Handwoven—you like them? Gifts to me from...friends."

Nice pocketbooks his friends had. She smiled

faintly. "They're quite unusual." What did he want with her?

"Would you care for something to drink?"

"Just water."

Hafner moved to the ornately carved bar in the corner of the huge room, glancing up at her in the mirror behind it. "You athletic types—so tiresome in your healthy tastes." He poured her a sparkling water, himself a Scotch.

Jillian looked around at the size of the room and how far they were from the door. She wanted out of here in the worst way, but then she wouldn't know what he planned for Cullinane. She had to find out more.

Forcing herself to settle back on the overstuffed black leather sofa, Jillian didn't let herself flinch when Hafner sat down beside her, handing her the water.

"Thank you." She drank thirstily, eyeing him over her glass, remembering another day when he'd watched her drinking water and traced the moisture down her throat.

Don't press your luck, Hafner.

He seemed to be thinking of that time, too, but he didn't touch. He just watched, his eyes greedily following a drop of sweat she could feel rolling down her chest, sliding into the valley between her breasts.

The eyes of a predator, waiting to pounce.

"Tell me, Jillian." He spoke lazily, setting his glass down on the smoked-glass table in front of them. Reaching into his pocket, he drew out his knife, examining it slowly, then glancing up at her. "What do you think of our Cullinane?"

She was mesmerized by the knife as though by a

snake ready to strike, and it took her a minute to tear her gaze away. "I don't know what you mean."

"How would you describe him to someone new?"

"You mean his appearance?"

His eyes reproved her. "Come now, dear, let's don't play games."

Yeah, right. The game player didn't want to play games. Drawing a deep breath, she began her list. "I'd have to say that he's strong, very intelligent, that I'd never play poker with him—"

Hafner laughed. "Oh, I do like you, my dear. But what about loyalty? Would you include that in the list of Cullinane's virtues?"

Was this a test? Smiling disingenuously, she continued, "Yes, along with stubborn, single-minded, arrogant..."

Hafner laughed again, then opened the knife and began cleaning his nails, falling silent and staring at the far wall as though she weren't even in the room.

After a long moment in which Jillian sat very still, knowing she must keep her wits about her, he finally turned and spoke, his tone casual. But his words were not.

"And to whom are you loyal, Jillian?"

She felt pinned, frozen—all but staked out on the ground by the power of that lazy, merciless gaze. "I work for you."

Holding up one finger, knife waving in the air, he addressed the room. "Notice that she didn't say she was loyal to me. But never mind that." Hafner swung his head around, his gaze burning into her. "If I were to assign you to help me with a little matter, would you feel compelled to report it to Cullinane?"

"I don't work for Cullinane."

"You report to him."

"But you pay the bills."

Hafner smiled, as if she were a bright student. "I do, don't I? Pity Cullinane often forgets that." Musing, he stared across the room once more.

"There is an important shipment coming in tomorrow. I may need your services. Has Cullinane given you an assignment?"

Tomorrow? He'd told her a week—it had been only three days. Mind whirling, she hesitated almost too long.

"Jillian?"

"Uh, no. Nothing specific yet." *What game are you playing, Cullinane? What about trust?*

"Curious," he mused. "But then, this will be your first. Perhaps he prefers to keep you here to watch the compound. But be that as it may, I want you to do something for me—"

A loud knock sounded at the door.

"Just a moment," Hafner called out, his annoyance clear. Grasping her chin in his hand, he studied her closely with those pale, soulless eyes. "You fascinate me so, Jillian. I want—"

Caught in his gaze, she could barely repress a shudder. He didn't just repulse her; something in him chilled her to the bone.

The knocking cracked like gunfire the second time. Hafner sighed and rose. Crossing the room, he turned a lock she hadn't noticed and swung the door open to reveal an unsmiling Cullinane, his gaze scanning the room and quickly finding her.

He stilled, glaring. Both relieved and annoyed by

the interruption, Jillian glared back. For one brief second she saw a flicker of another emotion behind the mask of stone.

"I'm busy, Cullinane," Hafner snapped.

"So I see. You have a phone call."

"Since when are you the messenger boy?"

"This one's important. In the library." Cullinane turned his stare back to her.

Casting a glance loaded with meaning back at her, Hafner sighed. "We'll talk later, Jillian." He left the room, but Cullinane remained, filling the doorway with his dark, brooding presence.

Jillian settled back on the cushions, just to nettle him. So they were back to playing games.

Cullinane's gaze dismissed her. "Come on, Jillian. Hafner doesn't like anyone in his rooms when he's not here."

"I don't think he'll mind."

His gaze snapped back to her. "But I will."

"I don't particularly care what you mind."

His jaw flexed. "Please leave, Jillian."

Suddenly furious at his high-handed treatment of her, she leapt up from the sofa and marched up to him, hissing, "You lied to me. It's tomorrow."

He glanced toward the hall. "Not now." His voice low and urgent, he all but whispered. "Later. I'll talk to you later."

Then she saw the strain of the days on him. What must it be like to be this close to the end of two years undercover? She was clawing to get out after only a flicker of the time.

He was right. She would have it out with him later. But not here. Not now. Tony was likely still nearby.

She wouldn't endanger Cullinane, no matter how he upset her.

But they would talk. She wanted answers. She had to plan.

In the darkness of his room Cullinane paced, details of tomorrow's operation whirling in his head. He would try to make himself sleep later, but sleep was not on the agenda right now.

He still had to deal with Jillian; she wouldn't like his plan. Worried about some way to get Alice and Mary Beth away from the compound without alerting Hafner, he'd decided that Jillian made the most likely candidate to spirit them away. Since she and the family had become such friends, it would not necessarily arouse anyone's suspicions for Jillian to take them shopping, since Alice rarely drove anywhere. Thank goodness the other kids would be in school.

Jillian wouldn't like it, and it would also rob him of her help to watch Hafner, but he'd watched his own back for years. Sending her away with Alice and Mary Beth would accomplish two important needs for him: to safeguard innocents and to keep Jillian away from Hafner. That he also wanted Jillian safe was not an argument she would appreciate, but nonetheless, he felt it, however Neanderthal that made him.

They'd decided on a morning raid, since with the exception of Alice's family, Jillian and himself, the compound was slow to awaken each day. Hafner slept very late; he would be sluggish and easier to command. With any luck, he would fall right into their plan to keep up the pretense of Cullinane's job as security chief. In the case of a raid, Cullinane had made contingency plans as part of his job. The first order of business was to get Hafner out of the compound.

Cullinane would follow the plan, separating Hafner from the rest of the men. The men would let him go, expecting Cullinane to act in that manner; they'd practiced it many times. They wouldn't balk at him leaving to take Hafner to a safe house. Once he'd left with Hafner, they would all be rounded up.

He would head to Houma, to the fishing camp, a place Hafner felt comfortable. But waiting there would be other agents, ready to arrest Hafner. Cullinane would be caught in the sweep; a cover that had taken more than two years to build wasn't cast away lightly. It could still be needed later.

Meanwhile, a third contingent of the task force would be boarding shrimp boats and seizing the contraband, while the overseas busts went on, as well.

A great plan. It ought to work. But Cullinane had been at this game too long to believe it would be that simple. Even if he didn't have Jillian to worry about, a thousand things could still go wrong.

And he did have Jillian to worry about—the first order of business, getting her to go along with a plan she would hate.

A plan that neatly removed her from the action.

Running impatient fingers through his hair, Cullinane stared out into the darkness, composing arguments he hoped would sway the most determined woman he'd ever met.

He was so close. He was so tired.

So much was at stake.

Chapter Fourteen

Jillian prowled the boundaries of her room. Where was he? He'd said he would come to her later, to talk about tomorrow. It was already later, and no sign of him yet. Jillian decided she'd give him a few more minutes, then she was headed toward his rooms to beard the lion in his den.

Torn between anger and unease, she paced, thinking about tomorrow. She'd been on raids before, of course, but never anything of this magnitude. Cullinane was FBI, but likely there would be ATF and the Coast Guard involved, perhaps the DEA and local authorities. A lot of people involved; a lot to go wrong.

She'd hoped Hafner would approach her and give her another chance to find out his plans regarding Cullinane, but he'd been gone all evening. With no idea how he would try to involve her, she'd just have to stay alert, watch him closely while keeping an eye out for danger threatening Cullinane. She had her weapon; she had her skills. She would be all right—she just had to stay loose, remain observant.

And she had to pry details out of Mr. Granite.

Jillian stopped, staring out her window at silhouetted treetops against the glow of security lighting. She had a lot to think about, but Cullinane had much more.

Remembering the edgy excitement, the dread and nerves she'd always felt before a raid, Jillian wondered what Cullinane must be feeling now, with so many years of his life on the line. Her anger faded in the light of her worry. He must be strung pretty tightly tonight. Even a stone man couldn't keep it all at bay.

You don't know how much I want him…nothing short of dying will stop me from taking him down. His words returned to her, the haunted shadows in his eyes alive in her memory. Yes, Cullinane had to be feeling this night deeply. She didn't know why, but this was personal for him, too. They just differed on their solutions to the problem of Hafner.

She would go to him, but she would be calm; she would listen. She'd been so caught up in her own feelings that she hadn't stopped to consider how this all weighed down on him. He had a lot to juggle, even without the threat to his life—or the complication of her single-mindedness.

But Belinda—

Jillian shook her head. She thought about Cullinane, about what was good and strong between them—about how much she wanted it to live and grow and thrive.

Maybe Hiroshi was right. Maybe it was time to let Belinda go. Forgiveness would not come easily, if it ever came at all. She had let her sister down when Belinda had needed her most.

But was that the legacy Belinda would have wanted? Jillian's life, like her own, destroyed in one violent act? She realized then how much she wanted to be free of this cloud, this darkness that had ruled her life ever since she'd received the call that Belinda was dead.

She'd made a mistake, a big one, with her sister. But she thought about Cullinane's voice, the longing she'd heard there, and she knew that he would do his best to see Hafner punished.

But he was doing it the right way, the hard way. Cullinane was right. Shooting Hafner down in cold blood, though it might be quick and easy, would not only ruin her life, it would steal something from her soul. And now she had something more important to live for—the man who cared enough to give her a chance at a life she'd only dreamed of before.

She found she wanted that chance, wanted to make something positive of Belinda's loss. She didn't know what that might be yet, but she recognized the first step.

Tonight, Cullinane just might need a friend.

Making her way down the hall, she tapped softly at his door.

"It's not locked." She barely heard his voice, muffled by the door. Slowly she pushed it open.

He leaned against the window across the room,

looking out, his strong profile somehow weary and troubled. He spoke without turning, his voice low and somber. "Hello, Jillian."

"How could you be sure it was me? A little risky, don't you think, leaving it unlocked?"

He smiled faintly and shook his head, turning his face to her. "I'd have bet the farm on seeing you tonight."

"I'm so predictable?"

He chuckled, pushing away from the window and moving toward her, shaking his head again. "No, you're that stubborn and determined. I knew if I didn't come to you, you'd show up here, demanding answers." Coming to a stop before her, he looked down, eyes glowing silver, shadowed but somehow fond.

Jillian stared at his lips, realizing she wanted to feel his kiss once again. Wanted to reach up and cradle his head against her, to soothe the lines of worry from his brow.

She did neither. "Would I have gotten my answers?"

He held her gaze, then his dropped to her lips. "The ones I'm free to give." His voice was quiet and sad—and weary.

Jillian suddenly wanted to forget all that kept them apart, all the reasons they were at odds. For just a little span of time, she wanted to give this noble man the gift of her silence, her support.

Tomorrow might bring anything—there could be sorrow and pain, even death. When her heart seized at the thought of his strong heart ceasing to beat, she reached up and placed one hand on his chest, reassured by the quickening thump beneath her fingers.

They might never have any more than this. There were no guarantees; she knew too well how cruel fate could be. Whatever hadn't been resolved between them would still be there tomorrow, but for now, she thought he'd been alone long enough. Two years was a long time in the belly of the beast.

Lifting her gaze to his, she saw his own filled with questions.

"Jillian, I can't—"

"Shh." She placed her fingers over his lips. "I'm not asking for anything you can't give. Just one more taste of the magic, Cullinane. I need it—I think you do, too."

"Drake." His voice low and urgent, his eyes appealed. "My name is Drake Morgan. For just tonight, I'd like to hear my own name."

Her heart squeezed. So long alone. Pressing herself closer, rising to her toes, she pulled his head down to hers. "I want this night with you. No duty, no obligations, no one else but us. This one night, Drake. It might be all we ever have."

Drake pulled her close almost roughly, kissing her with all the urgency he felt. It might be utter insanity, but she was right—this could be all they ever had. He'd done all he could to take care of tomorrow.

He wanted this night, too. Needed it, needed *her* with an urgency that bordered on madness.

He pulled his mouth away, already aching to return. "Tell me, Jillian," he whispered. "Tell me how you want me to touch you. I don't want you to ever forget this night."

Tears he'd never thought to see from this strong, self-contained woman shimmered, threatening to spill. He felt them in his gut; he wanted to drink them from her lashes, to bathe away her pain with his tongue. A tenderness stole over him, a tenderness he'd never known until he'd met this remarkable woman—until he'd seen her pride, her refusal to accept defeat, her valor in facing down incredible odds.

"No, let me, Drake. Let me be the one. For too long you've been alone." Stepping back only slightly, she took his hand and led him to the bed, pulling him down on it, then rising over him, her eyes soft and warm. "Let me make love to you tonight, Drake Morgan. Just relax—and feel my touch."

Relax. When Jillian touched him, relaxation was the last thing on his mind. Drake nearly laughed, but just then her fingers reached out to stroke his face, to slide into his hair, gently massage his scalp. Her slow, teasing touch soothed, calmed—aroused. He reached up to drag her down to him, needing to feel her close, but Jillian laughed and pinned his wrists at his shoulders, eyes sparkling in challenge.

"Oh, no, you don't. This is my show for now." The smile he'd seen too seldom now gleamed with mischief. "Don't make me have to hurt you, Drake." For emphasis, she rubbed herself over him where she straddled his groin.

He grinned. They both knew he could get free in an instant. She was strong, but he was stronger. No question, though, that being in the unaccustomed position of submission was erotic. She could have her way with him; he'd get even later.

Then rational thought deserted him with the first

rake of her nails at the opening of his shirt. Eyes sparkling, she grasped his shirt in both hands and ripped it open, buttons flying across the bed. Drake felt his body leap beneath her, and gritted his teeth not to flip her over and drive within the sweet warm promise he knew was waiting.

The tests didn't end there. Relax, hell. Jillian was bent on driving him out of his mind.

He didn't care. Jaw flexing, he sucked in a breath at the feel of her silky hair brushing his chest, her hot mouth searching out tender places he'd never known he had. When she sucked at his nipple, biting lightly with her teeth, he almost came off the bed. Jerking his hands up to grab her hair, he dragged her mouth to his.

Drake rolled to bring her under him, but Jillian resisted, pulling her mouth away from his, her breathing heavy, her lips swollen from his kiss. With eyes that promised dark delights, she shook her head.

"Oh, no, stone man." With a wicked smile she lifted herself and closed her hand around the straining length of him. "I'm not finished with you yet."

Drake groaned and bucked beneath her. "Jillian..." he warned.

One delicate brow arched. "I wouldn't make idle threats, if I were you." Her playful smile warned— and promised. Fingers reached for the waist of his jeans, nimble fingers that slid beneath buttons, stealing mind-clawing touches of the heated flesh surging beneath. With each button, his mind slipped further away, his control weakening, his will scorched by fingers of flame.

When his buttons were mostly open and his mind

mostly gone, she placed long, slender fingers beneath the waistband of his briefs, sliding the fabric so slowly he thought he might have to resort to force to make her end his agony.

But she merely smiled, her heated gaze understanding every bit of the cost she exacted. Licking her lips slowly, making him groan and strain against her hand, Jillian lowered her head and took him in her mouth, fiery silk brushing his belly.

Drake growled, thrusting into the warm, wet heaven. "Jillian—if you want anything left, you'd—" He sucked in a breath as she pulled away, her tongue licking slowly up his length. He bit back a groan.

Lifting her head, Jillian smiled, the smile of a woman who knows her power. Running her tongue over her lips, she stroked him with one hand, rising up over him to press his shaft against the heat of her, eyes glowing with desire.

Drake grabbed her and rolled, bringing her beneath him so fast, her eyes widened in surprise. "That's all she wrote, woman. It's my turn now."

With the same lack of care she'd shown for his shirt, Drake jerked her blouse open, scattering the second shower of buttons.

Jillian laughed, low and throaty, her eyes issuing a challenge.

God, he loved this woman! He pushed away the quick stab of sadness, knowing they had only tonight. She was his perfect mate—his equal, his tormentor, his completion.

No one could ever match her. They might have

only tonight, but he'd give her the best of himself in these stolen hours.

Unhooking the scrap of lace over her breasts, Drake stopped and admired. He knew the feel of these breasts, could already feel the weight of them in his hands. Slowly, reverently, he placed one hand over each, the feel of her heated skin shocking his palms.

Jillian arched against him, her hips rocking toward his groin. He fought to restrain himself, to make this last forever, if he could. Still holding the tender fullness in his hands, he lowered his mouth to bathe her lips with a slow stroke of his tongue.

As though in answer, Jillian's lips parted, but he didn't claim them yet. Instead, he teased her with light, flickering strokes at the corners, tickling the sensitive skin just bordering her lips. Jillian sucked in a breath but remained very still, her body quivering slightly, her eyes opening to watch him.

For such a fierce woman, she was oddly almost shy, her delight in his touch hesitant and surprised. Wanting somehow to reach her, to let her know what she meant, he brought his hands up to cradle her face.

"You are precious to me, Jillian Blake," he vowed, knowing he'd never say that to anyone else. She was unique, a treasure he wanted to keep and to cherish for a long time to come. If only fate would let him.

Her whiskey eyes melted, moisture shimmering over the surface. He could see the war within them, the same longing he felt to have done with the battles, with all that divided them.

A small remnant of reason tugged at him, reminding him with hateful clarity that his soul was not his to give to her—not this night. Dreaded duty and responsibility reared their ugly heads; Drake tamped them down, promises rendered, heart once again heavy.

The time for teasing was gone. They still had battles to fight, but the need within him called out. He could not forget tomorrow.

But for now, it was still the night.

Need pushing him onward, he sought to draw her soul out of her body to mate it with his. He used every means at his disposal to call to her, to bring her to him. As he stripped them both with abandon, Drake's craving to feel her grew, until at last he could press bare skin to bare skin, heart to heart.

He could hear the catch in Jillian's breath, feel the rise of her breast against his mouth. He teased and appealed, willing her closer, drawing every last nerve to tingling need. He wanted her as desperate for him as he was for her.

Jillian felt his sorrow, felt the change sweep over him. Where playfulness had reigned, now deep, fevered need took its place. But the need dwelled within her, as well; she heeded his call.

"Come to me, Jillian. Let me have all of you," he whispered, his heated breath stirring the tender flesh at her core. His fevered caresses, the strokes of his tongue, lashed her higher and higher, her nerves screaming for mercy. He was taking her beyond their night of magic, pulling her farther and farther from herself.

Heat flashed through her body, rippling beneath her skin. Just as she started to beg him to stop, convinced she'd reached her limit, Drake slid his tongue inside her, and she came apart, her whole body flaring white-hot. Her legs trembled, gooseflesh broke out on her skin. Breathless and spiraling, Jillian watched him rise above her, his dark beauty making her heart ache.

The silver eyes of the sorcerer gave way to the haunted gray velvet of a man in need. More naked than she'd ever seen, Drake's soul shone out from those eyes, asking for her care.

Jillian reached out her arms to him, still flying high, wanting with everything in her to hold him, to cherish him, to push away every barrier.

When he slowly entered her, filling her to aching completion, she felt the slow track of tears glide into her hair, her heart cracking in her chest.

For no matter that this was heaven, that this was where they both belonged—

No matter that she needed him desperately, and he needed her—

They still had to face tomorrow.

And each knew, only too well, that these might be the last, precious moments of goodbye.

Jillian stirred, and Drake tightened his arms around her, turning his face into her hair, breathing in her scent. He prayed that she wouldn't open her eyes yet, wouldn't awaken.

Once she did, the questions would begin.

And when that happened, he would have to begin pulling back, resume the mask of Cullinane and play games once again. He wished he could just tell her what he needed and know she'd comply, but he understood the power of Jillian's guilt, the strength of her sense of honor, her duty to her family.

He understood; he had demons of his own. Tiny voices, crying out for justice.

He could push her, could see if what they'd found together was strong enough to challenge the chains that bound her to her duty. But he was reluctant to put their own bond to such a test so soon. They had much more experience as foes; with love, they hadn't yet tested shaky newborn legs.

Love. He'd never thought it would be his lot, had given up the dream long ago. Lips curving slightly, he gazed down at the face of the woman he now knew he loved. Life certainly had its ironies. With the worst possible timing, after so many years alone, love had walked into his life in the form of a woman who tested him at every turn.

A woman he still wasn't sure he could trust.

It wasn't that Jillian was faithless or weak; on the contrary, her loyalties were so strong, her sense of responsibility so much a part of the very air she breathed, that it was those same virtues that would make it agonizing for her to choose between what she believed she owed those she cared for and what she might want for herself.

How could he not understand the struggle? It was his own.

So he would say nothing of love yet, though it might mean he never could. If he was lost in this battle today, he'd never get the chance. But his love for her was his burden, one he would not load upon slender shoulders that already carried too much weight. A precious burden he'd take with him into battle.

And having admitted it to himself, Drake felt both

fear and strength. Jillian filled up the hollow spaces inside him, the empty shell. Her vitality and spark lit up the dark corners of a soul long ago resigned to the cold. She fortified his strength. The fear came from at last having something to lose.

For a very long time he'd had a mission. He'd wanted to live to see it completed. But outside of that, Drake had had nothing to lose. His life was worth very little—there to sacrifice in the service of his duty but worth little to anyone else.

Jillian had changed all that. Now he wanted to live, to see where they could go. But even more than his own life, a chill fear invaded his heart at the thought of danger coming to her.

That's why he had to convince her to play this his way. More than his own life, he wanted to preserve hers. There were too many dangers lying in wait on this day, too many possibilities for her to be harmed. Though he knew very well she could take care of herself, still something within him needed to protect.

And the best way he could think of to accomplish that was to convince Jillian to leave the compound. He thanked his lucky stars for Alice and Mary Beth; Jillian would never leave on her own, but she might be persuaded to do it to protect them.

Just then she rolled closer, her face nuzzling into his throat, her warm breath tickling his skin.

"Drake?" she murmured sleepily.

"Shh," he whispered, drawing her closer into the circle of his arms. "It's not morning yet."

Sliding one hand across his belly, she snuggled closer. His body leapt in response to her nearness.

Drake fought back the urge to tilt her head back for a kiss, to lose himself inside her once more.

And then it was too late for loving. He felt her awakening.

Turning her face up to his, she rolled slightly away, pushing her hair away from her face, drowsy, whiskey brown eyes coming awake. "Hi," she murmured, smiling.

"Hi, yourself." He stroked her hair.

For one suspended moment, their eyes met in memory, in silent wonder at the power and magic of what they'd shared.

Then he could see awareness return, the shadows stealing back into her eyes as they stole over his heart.

"We don't have much time, do we?"

Drake shook his head, not trusting his voice.

"Drake—"

He placed a finger over her lips. "I know. And I think you'd better call me the old name. We can't afford a slip." But the moment she nodded, he felt his heart shiver against the cold. Cullinane was back; it was time to face the end.

"It's happening today, isn't it?" she asked.

"Yes." Forcing himself to face the reality, he went on. "In the morning. Before Hafner's up."

"Where do you need me?"

Here it came. He drew a deep breath. "I have one big worry that I can only trust you to handle."

Her look was solemn, but her eyes gleamed pleasure. "What is it?"

Sitting up against the headboard, he captured her gaze. "The other children will be gone to school, but Mary Beth will still be here—and Alice."

"You need me to watch them."

"I need you to take them away from the compound. Pretend you're driving Alice to the market and take Mary Beth with you."

Jillian's dark eyes narrowed. "You want me away from Hafner."

This is where it would get dicey. "No, that's not what I'm saying."

"But it's what you mean. You don't trust me not to take him out."

"Jillian, the trust has to go both ways. I promise you that Hafner will not go free, but I need your help. It's the one part of the plan I wasn't happy with because I had no way to send Alice and Mary Beth away without arousing suspicions and taking a chance on fouling everything up. I'd tried to resign myself to just making sure they stayed hidden, but it was still a risk. But this would work. Everyone here knows how close you've become to those children, and you and Alice have been very friendly. Alice doesn't drive herself much, so it's the perfect answer to be sure they're out of harm's way."

She frowned. "But what about Hafner? What about watching your back?"

"I'll be careful, but there's no one else I can trust to do this. The task force was alerted to watch out for Alice and the kids, but you know anything can happen in a raid."

"Which is why I should be here," she insisted.

He shook his head, clasping her shoulders. "I won't be here that long."

She eyed him carefully. "The contingency plan—

you're going to take Hafner out of here, just like we've practiced.''

Cullinane looked at her, mind racing. She hadn't exactly agreed, but she wasn't actively fighting him over this. If he hoped to convince her of how important her cooperation was and secure her agreement, he'd have to share this much of the plan with her. He nodded. ''I'm going to try. Will you help me?''

He could see the war going on inside her. She would chafe at being away from the action, but he wasn't kidding—this part of the plan had worried him. But given Alice's sense of obligation toward Hafner, she was too much of a wild card. He'd been prepared to lure her and Mary Beth to the security command center and lock them inside the extra-thick walls if it came to that. They would be safe there, but they would be safer completely away. Jillian's invitation to drive Alice to the market would be the perfect plan, arousing no suspicions on Alice's part. Ron did it often; Jillian would simply substitute.

Jillian looked away, obviously not happy about it, then glanced back. ''How sure are you that someone else will be watching out for you?''

''Very sure.'' In truth, he wasn't. Everyone on the task force had plenty else to do without guarding him. In reality, he would be on his own. The only watching would come from outside the walls until the raid actually began. He would be vulnerable to anything Hafner might have cooked up with the men inside the walls, but he'd have to hope that Hafner's paranoia would prevent him from using anyone Cullinane had hired and trained. He'd more likely use an outsider.

She almost smiled. "You knew I would hate this, didn't you?"

All he could do was nod.

"Damn you, Cullinane. You knew I couldn't risk them. Did you plan all this out ahead of time, in that serpentine mind of yours?"

He had to smile at that. "Nobody could plan for you, Jillian. You're the wild card that throws every operations planner into a cold sweat."

Her smile faded, shadows claiming her eyes. Glancing downward, she picked at the sheets, worrying the fabric.

"I'm afraid." Whiskey brown eyes rose to meet his, and he saw the fear rising. "I do trust you—but I don't trust fate. I've lost too many people I love, and I know how easily you could become one of that number."

He'd think later about how it shot through his system, the idea that she could love him. But right now he had to make sure she was safe. "I won't die, Jillian."

Tears brimmed, her face strained and pale. "You can't be sure of that." Bloodless, her fingers crushed the sheets in her fist.

He put his soul into his eyes and answered. "I'm not leaving you, Jillian—not when we've barely begun. You can take that to the bank. I'm coming out of this, and I'm coming straight to you."

She tried for a smile, but it died, stillborn.

There was nothing he could do but wait.

Finally she looked up at him, her gaze assessing, measuring how much she dared to believe. Sorrow washed over her face, sorrow…and resignation. "All right, you win. I'll do it your way."

The satisfaction he would have expected to feel didn't emerge. He didn't want it to be a contest. And only time would tell how much they would both lose.

But knowing that this had cost her, he reached out to interlace her fingers with his. Voice husky with emotions he couldn't share, Cullinane brought her fingers to his lips and spoke the only words he trusted himself to say. "Thank you."

Jillian's troubled gaze studied him as he felt her retreat. Tightening his fingers on hers, he willed her back.

"I should go to my room," she said quietly.

"I know." He kissed her fingers again. "We both need to sleep."

"Yes." She nodded. But she didn't move.

Turning her fingers around and covering her hand with his, he held on tightly. "I don't want this night to end."

Jillian looked at him sadly, knowledge of the widening rift there in her gaze. "It already has."

"No." He spoke fiercely, sudden determination taking over. He would hold back the dawn a little longer, just to hold her. "Stay with me, Jillian." Just a little longer. "I'll set the alarm so we'll get you out of here in plenty of time. But I want to sleep with you in my arms."

She wanted it, too, he could see that. But she understood that they were nearing the end. Finally he made the decision he wanted, turning to set the alarm for four-thirty. He heard the rustle of sheets behind him and wondered if he'd feel her weight leave the bed.

But instead he felt her arms come around him from behind, hugging his waist. Turning toward her, he took her down to the mattress, holding her close—so close he could feel their heartbeats mingling, keeping time with the sands of the hourglass that were slipping away.

She needed to sleep; he needed his rest. Tomorrow would be grueling and they would need to be in top form.

But somehow he knew that the feel of her would restore him more than sleep ever could. He would watch over her and hope she would rest.

In the heart of the darkness they would draw sustenance from each other, arm their souls against what was to come.

And together they would struggle in vain to hold back the dawn.

Chapter Fifteen

Why, Jillian? Why didn't you help me when I needed you? Look what you've done...not my sister...look what you've done—

"Jillian, wake up. It's only a dream."

Heart ramming against her chest, lungs burning as she clawed for air, Jillian gasped, scrambling to escape the restraints lashing her to the bed.

"Jillian, sweet." His deep voice rumbled, hand stroking her hair. "It's all right. You were only dreaming."

Drake. His arms held her down. She sagged in relief.

Shaking her head to clear it, Jillian pulled away, her mind still full of the horror of what she'd almost let slip away in the night.

Belinda.

Loretta.

Justice too long denied.

Shoving her hair away from her face, she rose to her knees, staring at him, struggling to reconcile what she'd done. For too many moments last night she'd let herself forget, let herself believe in something that she wanted desperately—an end to this mission, an end that would free her.

But her dream was a reminder, a wake-up call from her conscience. She'd known going in that they could have only this night, but she'd allowed herself to hope for more. Now she was bone-deep scared of the risk she was taking. Today she could lose both Drake and her chance at justice.

Drawing away from him while she still could, Jillian rose from the bed, unable to meet his eyes. Turning away, she searched for her clothes and began slipping them on.

"Jillian, look at me," his low, urgent tone commanded. "You're having second thoughts, aren't you?"

She closed her eyes, struggling to compose her features. Slowly she turned around, opening her eyes.

It hurt to look at him. His dark beauty stung her, raven hair falling around his powerful shoulders, the streak of silver like a badge of command. But it was the eyes that hurt her most, for they were still open to her, still reaching out. Haunted eyes, giving up secrets held close for years.

Suddenly she had to know.

"Why do you hate him? You do, don't you?"

The flash of pain answered. Slowly he nodded. "It was a long time ago. I was the assistant legal attaché to the embassy in Rome. I misread the signals, and the children of an orphanage in Rome died from a bomb he planted.'' His voice twisted. ''He and his terrorist buddies wanted some of their fellow scum released from prison. I don't think Hafner even stayed around to see the damage, probably never gave them a second thought. But I was there. I saw—'' He cleared his throat, then continued. ''I saw the results of my miscalculation. I'd played with those children, even thought about trying to adopt one or two. Instead I killed them because I made a mistake, underestimated Klaus Hafner. I swore then that someday I'd get him, that I'd redeem myself.''

As he lifted tortured eyes to hers, his voice grew hard. ''I've waited a long time for this, Jillian. Believe me when I say he won't escape his punishment.''

The sticky feel of Loretta's blood still marked her fingers, the dull ache of betraying Belinda still scraped at her heart. But Drake had his own pain, his own horrors that haunted him.

She understood better now, and she believed more than ever that he'd do his best to make it happen.

But could she be sure Hafner wouldn't walk away, ever again? Could she take a chance on a system that had failed more than once?

It came down to trust, just as he'd said. This was their defining moment. What happened next was up to her.

Crossing the carpet, she leaned down and poured her plea into one last, long, sweet kiss. When she felt his hands cradle her face, it was all she could do not to cry out in anguish.

"I believe in you, Drake—but I can't help being afraid. Hafner's suspicious, and he's a murderer. If anything happened to you, I'd never forgive myself." She'd seen his face when he'd said he would have backup, and she knew the truth. For precious minutes he would be totally alone and outnumbered.

"I have the training. I can help you. I'll leave Hafner alone, but please let me stay with you. I'll watch out for Alice and Mary Beth, but let me watch your back."

"I can't do that. Please, just help me. Please do what I ask."

She drew back and tried for a smile. The one that answered her was as sad as her own, as filled with longing and dark knowledge.

"Jillian, when this is over—" He stopped, then cleared his throat. "Don't come back here. Take Alice and Mary Beth to the motel where you were staying when you first came. Register under Loretta's name. I'll come to you as soon as I can."

And what if you're dead? How do I go on without you?

"All right," she whispered, feeling her heart all but torn from her chest. Turning away with effort, she walked to the door. She couldn't keep badgering him. He had so much on his mind, so much to coordinate. She ran the risk of endangering him just by making him worry about her when he needed to concentrate. But this was agony—she knew how to take responsibility, to take action. To step aside and give up control was terrifying.

She straightened, drawing a deep breath, speaking back over her shoulder. "You'd better come back to me safe and sound, Drake Morgan.'' Her voice cracked. ''Don't you make me bury you, too.'' Holding on to her composure with the tiniest of threads, she couldn't turn back to look at him. If she did, she would beg. Arms wrapped tight around her middle, Jillian left his room.

The night was over. The final day had begun.

Heaven help them both.

Drake toweled off after his shower, watching the monitors, seeing Jillian pull away in a sedan with Alice in the passenger seat, Mary Beth in the back. Though he'd wanted to speak to Jillian one last time, he'd denied himself that luxury—what could he say that would have any meaning?

He couldn't tell her yet that he loved her, and he couldn't promise it would all work out all right. So instead, he watched his dreams drive away, out of the compound.

But to safety, thank goodness. She only had to get a few hundred yards away before she would be into the ring controlled by the task force. He'd just returned from his run, preferring to keep his schedule normal, and had passed the unmarked vehicle around the curve where Alonzo sat waiting, the communications post behind him in the van. He hadn't broken stride, had merely nodded to signal that all was still as expected inside the compound.

It hadn't been his best workout, either on the road or in the gym, but he'd thanked his lucky stars that for once, Jillian hadn't shown up for hers.

He didn't think parting was any easier for her than for him.

But enough of that. He couldn't think about Jillian again until this was all over. Right now, a lot of lives depended upon him staying focused, getting this right.

He dressed slowly, still some time to spare. He didn't need to allow time to eat; he needed to be sharp, not sated. He'd always done better when he was a little edgy from hunger. Lean and mean, that was what the situation demanded.

Scanning the other monitors, he could see that so far, the men were all in their expected places inside the compound. Solly was still asleep—he'd pulled the late shift. Tony was headed toward the gym and Ron read the paper while eating his breakfast. Fred would be slowed by his cast, but he presented the greatest danger at the moment. He was in the command center, watching the bank of monitors there, staying in touch with the two men patrolling the grounds. Still convinced he had something to prove after Jillian had injured him, Fred wouldn't be likely to drop his guard.

Hafner, fortunately, still slept.

Finished dressing, Drake jammed his pistol in the back of his waistband, putting the extra magazine in one pocket of his jeans. He'd prefer to have the weapon securely holstered, but everyone in the compound had to believe that he'd been surprised by the raid, too. Details would register on the minds of these men he'd trained; he couldn't take anything for granted.

Glancing at the monitors again, he saw a cable company truck pull through the gate after Fred had cleared it from his post.

Showtime.

"Cullinane?" The intercom in his room crackled to life.

"Yeah?"

"Cable guy's here. Says you called them at Hafner's request." Fred's voice still sounded casual.

"Actually, Hafner wanted it for Alice. Said he thought she'd like to have an outlet in the kitchen. He's buying her a little TV for Christmas to put in there." His voice was cool and calm, his mind willing Fred to buy it.

"Got it. I'll buzz him in the back door."

"I'll be down in a minute and talk to him."

"Great."

Drake paced, watching the monitors, knowing he still had to wait, couldn't head for Hafner. On one screen, he saw Ron look up, nodding at the cable installer. He wished he could see inside the van, but the back had no windows.

Glancing at the screen that scanned the gate, Drake peered into the shadows, knowing men were spaced all around the outside, with a special concentration at the only entrance to the compound.

Movement on the kitchen monitor caught his gaze. Ron leapt up, his chair falling backward, orange juice flying from the glass in his hand. At that moment the back door burst open.

Within seconds the intercom in his room crackled to life. "Cullinane, we're being hit—Ron's down—" Fred's voice rose.

"I see it—I'm on my way to Hafner. Proceed to contingency number two." Without waiting for an answer, he sprinted down the hall to Hafner's rooms and burst in.

"Klaus! Get up, now!" He actually didn't care if he got Hafner away, but he had to make this look good, and they'd all agreed it would serve his cover best if he managed to make it out with Hafner in tow.

Hafner sat up quickly, blinking and covering his eyes.

"Up—now, Klaus, we're under attack. Get yourself dressed. You've got one minute."

They had cleared the gates of the compound now, and Jillian's every nerve strained to go back, to be with Drake.

Suddenly Alice leaned forward. "What's going on? Why are all these cars—?" she began, staring at the array of vehicles, all government issue.

"I don't know, but I'm sure Cullinane will be checking." Jillian tried to keep her voice light and neutral. *There's no one else I can trust to do this.* Drake's voice resounded in her head.

She couldn't let him down.

"Oh, no!" Alice's hand flew up to cover her mouth. "They're dressed in SWAT gear. Stop the car, Jillian. Turn around—we have to go back. I have to warn Klaus."

"No, Alice, we have to keep going." *Dear God, what if they mess this up? Drake's alone in there.* Her fingers tightened on the wheel, her knuckles going white with her need to go back, to make sure he was safe.

Alice's body went rigid. "Turn around, Jillian. Please."

Mary Beth began to whimper.

Jillian gritted her teeth and drove on until a man stepped into the road and held up a hand.

Alice's hand was on the door handle. "I'm going back. Please take care of Mary Beth for me."

Jillian's hand shot out to grab her arm. "Don't you know what Klaus does to make his money? This is your chance to be free."

Alice's face fell, tears springing into her eyes. "I don't want to know." Glancing back up at Jillian, she begged, "I can't just leave Klaus. I owe—"

"He deals in death, Alice. He's responsible for the deaths of too many people. You owe him nothing." She struggled to soften a voice turned harsh and bitter. "You owe it to yourself not to ruin your life."

Bingo, Jillian. Just what Drake told you.

Alice's eyes were confused, her suffering palpable.

"If you won't think of yourself, think of your kids."

Then the man reached her door. Jillian rolled down her window. "Ma'am, Agent Davis of the FBI. I'm going to have to search your vehicle."

Mary Beth's plaintive wail sounded from the back seat. Alice was stiff in the seat beside Jillian, seeming not to hear her.

Jillian had to get them out of there, but she couldn't speak frankly in front of Alice, in case Alice managed to escape. "Yes, sir. May I step out?"

"Slowly and carefully, hands above your head."

"Jillian, I—"

"It will be all right, Alice. Just stay put." She opened the door and stepped out, whispering so Alice couldn't hear. "Please, I have to talk to you. It's about Drake Morgan. He's in danger."

The agent looked down at her, bushy dark eyebrows pulled together. "Who are you?"

"Jillian Blake. He sent me out with the woman and child to keep them out of harm's way. But he's alone in there, and he could be hurt."

"Step over this way, please." Other agents took Alice and her daughter from the car and began searching it.

Jillian's temper exploded. "There's no time for this. You've got to listen to me—Hafner's suspicious of Drake. He's got something planned and I couldn't find out what it is. Drake wouldn't let me stay to help him—you've got to make sure he's not hurt."

"I'll ask the other woman—"

"No." She grabbed his arm without thinking. The men around him snapped to attention. Jillian forced herself to step back, to take a deep breath. "I'm sorry, but you have to listen to me. She's Hafner's sister and she wants to warn him that you're out here. She's not involved, as far as I know—she just wants to warn him because he's her brother. But Drake's in danger in there—who's watching his back?"

"We have everything under control. Agent Morgan is good at his job. Now, move over there. I'll have you escorted away from the scene, along with the woman and the girl, as soon as possible."

"No." She started to grab him again, then jerked her hand back. "I—please don't make me leave. Take them somewhere, but let me stay here. I can't leave him until I know—"

"Jillian Blake?" A new voice intruded.

She turned to see a tall man approaching. His dark

eyes scrutinized her carefully, but something in his gaze seemed more receptive than Agent Davis.

"I'm Special Agent Alonzo, Drake's case officer. What are you' saying about him? What kind of danger?"

Relief flooded through her. Maybe this man would listen. "I want to go back in there. If Alice and Mary Beth are safe, then I've done what I promised Drake. I want to go back."

The older agent shook his head. "That's not possible. You're a civilian."

"But I know the place, know the plan. I could make sure…"

His expression didn't budge. "You are not going back in there. Drake Morgan has been in a lot of tight spots before and no one in the Bureau can handle himself better. Now, tell me everything you know that might help him. We don't have much time."

Jillian, the trust has to go both ways. Please do what I ask.

She dragged in a deep breath and began to quickly outline everything she knew.

"All right, let's go." Drake sprinted through the concealing shrubbery toward the separate garage where a Jeep was kept, fueled and ready for just such an emergency.

"Stop, Cullinane."

Behind him, he heard Hafner breathing heavily. *That's what happens with too much of the good life, Klaus. You get soft.*

Then Hafner's voice changed, settled. "I said, stop, Cullinane."

Drake knew before he even turned what had happened. He thought about taking off, but before he could do anything, in his peripheral vision he spotted Solly and a man he'd never seen before approaching, weapons aimed right at him.

Slowly he turned, his mind racing. Hafner closed in on him, pale eyes gone cold. As Drake searched for a way out, one part of his mind went to the night just past, the promises he'd made about their future.

I'm sorry, Jillian.

"Your weapon, Cullinane, on the ground. Hurry up—I'm a little pressed for time."

"Klaus—"

The deadly blade of Hafner's knife clicked open. "Save it, Cullinane. Now before I kill you, why don't you tell me what's really going on?"

Jillian sat in the communications van, clasping her hands tightly between her knees, right foot jiggling as she tried to keep from crawling out of her skin.

He was in there, and forces were headed his way. But was he still alive? Had Hafner already taken action?

She'd never done anything harder than sitting there, waiting to find out if the man she loved was dead or alive—

Love. She did love him—desperately, she realized. No matter that they'd only known each other a short time and spent much of that as opponents—she loved Drake Morgan. She wanted a chance to explore that love, to find out if he felt anything similar.

She wanted to know Drake out from under the shadows of obligations and duties and pulse-pounding terror. Wanted to walk with him and spend quiet moments, wanted to know what he ate for breakfast, what he liked to read—

The radio squawked, interrupting her thoughts.

"We're inside now. Situation under control inside the house but there's movement at the far corner. Alpha team, what's your situation?"

A low voice sounded. "We were headed toward the wing where Morgan said they'd exit. I hear voices coming our way. Ten yards or less, sir."

The hush in the van pressed upon her. Jillian struggled to breathe, her pulse pounding so hard it roared in her ears.

Alonzo's grave face told her he felt it, too.

The voice came again in a whisper. "They've got the drop on him, sir. Morgan's being held at gunpoint by two men. Hafner's got a knife and he's very close to Morgan."

"Do you have the shot?" Alonzo's voice was steady.

"Not yet. Morgan's between us and Hafner. Stand by."

Oh, God…they're going to kill him. Just like Belinda, I'm going to lose Drake to Hafner. I shouldn't have left. I should be with him now. Jillian bowed over, wrapping her arms around her chest, trying to keep the grinding ache at bay.

But she knew…she already knew she'd lose him.

"Damn." The shout echoed. "Morgan's—"

Gunfire erupted, and Jillian couldn't stifle the keening moan that clawed its way from her throat.

"Man down!" the voice shouted, then all was chaos. More shots echoed.

Jillian leapt up, not waiting to hear more, just knowing that she had to see Drake again, had to be with him if he was the one hit. *Please God, let him be alive. Please don't take him from me so soon.* Alonzo shouted from behind her, but she used the evasive moves she'd learned and dodged capture, grabbing for the door handle and leaping out of the van.

She rounded the curve, staring toward the gate. Between her and the gate was the last wave of forces, pulling back as Fred, Ron and Tony were brought out of the compound. She started running, desperate to know, to be there with Drake. Shouts followed her, along with the pounding of footsteps. She could barely hear for the sound of her own sobs.

The crowd parted. A tall figure emerged, surrounded by a cluster of agents.

Jillian skidded to a stop, heart racing.

Then the figure straightened, shaking his head. Long dark hair—and a streak of silver. He came to a stop, staring at Jillian.

I'm coming out of this, and I'm coming straight to you.

Drake smiled, then he started moving toward her.

Jillian's heart soared; she broke into a run, suddenly feeling lighter than air. When they met, Drake's arms fastened around her, squeezing her so tightly she could barely breathe.

She didn't care. Wrapping her arms around his neck, she felt him lift her off the ground. Tears squeezed from her eyelids as she sobbed, "Thank God…oh, Drake, I thought I'd lost you. I love you— I love you so much. I was so afraid…."

Drake whispered in her ear. "I love you, too, Jillian Blake." His voice went hoarse. "When Hafner came after me while his men held me at gunpoint, all I could think was how much I wanted to come back to you—and how grateful I was that you were out of harm's way." He sat her down and searched her gaze. "Thank you for that. You did what I asked. You trusted me."

He smoothed back her hair, his face solemn. "Hafner's dead, Jillian. One of the snipers shot him when I broke his hold. The other men are in custody, one of them wounded."

Hafner was dead. The force that had driven her for so long was suddenly gone. Jillian tried to absorb what that meant—how much her life had changed in that instant.

"Is that—does that ruin everything for you?"

"No." He shook his head. "I don't think so. One of the agents back there told me they've already rounded up several key players overseas and the shrimp boats have been boarded. Right now, I don't even care. You're here and safe—we're both alive. That's all that matters to me."

"Oh, Drake, I was so scared when I heard they had you. I thought—"

"You were sorry you hadn't stayed and tried to kill Hafner, weren't you?"

Moisture blurred her vision. She shoved a hand roughly across her eyes, returning her gaze to his. "You were right, though." She shook her head. "I don't know if I could have done it." She glanced away. "Or if I had, I don't know if I could have lived with myself. I just didn't know how else—" Jillian exhaled roughly. "Nobody cared that she was gone but Loretta and me. And when Loretta couldn't pull out of her despair, and I knew it was my fault that—"

"Shh," he soothed, pulling her close again. "The important question now is, can you let her go? Can you forgive yourself for not being there to save her?" He stroked her hair. "Belinda was a grown woman, Jillian, making her own choices. You can only do so much for the people you love and then it's up to them." He leaned back. "And I'm telling you, after living with Hafner for two years and seeing his life-style, I can promise you it could be very seductive. In all likelihood, by the time you knew what she was doing, she was already in over her head."

"But I should have..." Her heart squeezed painfully.

"The cruelest words in the English language—'could have' and 'should have'—but it's always too late by the time we use them." He stroked her cheek. "Let her go, Jillian. Honor her memory by the way you go on from here. That's really all any of us can do."

Jillian searched his eyes, healing tears rolling down her cheeks. Then she buried her face against his chest and held on tight, her body shaking.

She couldn't believe how free she felt. It was stunning, realizing that she didn't have to always be in control. After so many years of being responsible, after the lonely months when her whole life seemed centered around vengeance, the sheer relief of having him to lean on was breathtaking. The knowledge that they might have a future together electrified her.

For long moments they stood there, drawing sustenance from simply holding one another.

Drake just held her, stroking her back, knowing he had to listen to his own advice. This operation was over, and he knew now he would never go back undercover. He was burned out; he wanted to move on. He had to say goodbye to the children who'd haunted his dreams for so long.

Jillian's voice was muffled by his chest. "It's really over, isn't it?" She raised tear-swollen eyes to his face. "We're free."

Caressing her hair, he wondered what that meant for them. His throat tight, he nodded. "What now, Jillian? Would you consider staying with a broken-down undercover agent?"

She gave him the first genuine smile he'd ever seen from her, faint but free of shadows and secrets. "It might have escaped your attention—" her voice was wavery, but her smile widened "—but you've already tried every trick in the book to drive me away. I haven't noticed you having much success. Got any more up your sleeve?"

Drake shook his head, his heart lightening. "I'm fresh out of ideas."

"Good." She pulled his head toward her, her breath soft on his face, her gaze filled with wonder. "Oh, lordy, Drake—we're really free." Kissing him hard and quickly, she pulled back suddenly, her eyes wide and glowing. "I feel…lighter."

"Me, too." Then his grin faded. "I'm finished with this, Jillian. I'm burned out. I don't know where I'll go from here. You're not getting any bargain. I'd understand if you wanted to back out." He studied her, waiting.

"Forgotten already how much I love a challenge?" Jillian's face broke into a grin filled with mischief. She crossed her arms over her chest. "Come on, big guy. Try and make me leave."

Heart lighter, he swung her up in his arms, lowering his mouth to hers. "I knew you were trouble the moment I laid eyes on you, Marshall."

"Like calls to like, hotshot—isn't that what you said?"

Their laughter was swallowed up in the heat of the kiss.

Epilogue

Six months later

Drake looked down from the ladder, watching Jillian and J.T. scuffle playfully, dueling with their paint scrapers. Shaking his head, he grinned. "You know, we'd have the center ready a lot sooner if you two would work for a change."

J.T. glanced up guiltily; Jillian just stuck out her tongue. "Party pooper. We're just taking a little break."

Adam piped up. "Then that's the third break in the last half hour. Rabbit and I are almost finished with our wall."

Drake glanced over and smiled. Rabbit shot him a quick smile, a different boy from the one they'd first met. Alice had dug past the bravado, finding a kid who had no one. Just as she'd taken charge of her own children, she'd taken on Rabbit as though he were another one of hers. Once she'd stepped out of Klaus's shadow, she'd amazed them all. She'd found the strength to take her children in hand, and the troubled boys had responded well.

Drake turned back, winking. "Yeah, Adam. Sometimes I wonder who the mature brother is."

J.T. frowned and turned back to his work. "Come on, Jillian. Quit fooling around. They're making us look bad."

Drake climbed down from the ladder where he'd just installed the fluorescent fixture on the ceiling. Walking up behind Jillian, he taunted, "Yeah, Jillian, quit fooling around." When she whirled around, protest ready, he scooped her up and threw her over his shoulder, crossing the room to the accompaniment of giggling girls and hooting boys—and Jillian's laughter as she beat on his back.

Walking through the kitchen past Loretta and Alice, both working hard on making it livable, he grinned at their raised eyebrows and kept walking. "Nice work, ladies."

Loretta's smile warmed his heart. She'd come a long way from the pale, thin woman he'd first met. Like them all, the idea of this center for troubled kids had given Loretta a mission.

He'd been surprised when Jillian had wanted to stay in Louisiana and bring Loretta here, thinking that this place would have held too many bad memories. But he should have realized that Jillian's sense of responsibility would extend to Alice and her kids. Jillian, whose own family had been decimated, seemed driven to create a new one out of whatever ragtag elements she found. Single mothers, gang members, burned-out former FBI agents—she wasn't particular. That same ferocious will she'd applied to hunting down Hafner she'd now turned on his idea of trying to help troubled kids avoid taking Belinda's path—or the one he'd come very close to taking in his own troubled youth.

Thanks to Hafner's generous life-style, Drake had had two years to add to his savings with the back pay he hadn't needed to spend. He'd taken retirement and sunk his nest egg into this place, an old convent school with a separate house on the grounds, where he and Jillian and their unconventional family would live.

Jillian wiggled on his shoulder, pulling his shirttail out of his jeans and slipping one hand down inside, caressing his behind.

He grinned. "Stop that. You're not supposed to be fooling around. Remember?"

"Let me down." Her voice breathy, she all but purred. "I promise I'll be good."

The promise in her voice went straight to his groin. In six months he still hadn't taken the edge off his craving for her. Entering the room they were sharing until they could get to fixing up their little house, he pulled her over his shoulder and dropped her on her back on the bed, shutting the door with his foot.

Balancing on his arms over her, one knee on the bed, he tried to look stern. "You're a hard case, Mrs. Morgan. Being good is something Loretta assures me you never really tried to master." But in truth, he delighted in every carefree smile, every mischievous look on her face. She'd finally let go of her ghosts.

"I promise. Cross my heart." She performed the motion over her heaving chest, her wedding band catching the light. Her color still high, her eyes darkened with longing, sparkling with challenge. "Come on, hotshot, wanna make me? We could leg-wrestle or something," she teased. "See who's the champion and who cries 'uncle' first."

"You're a bloodthirsty wench, you know that? Always spoiling for a challenge." Drake shook his head, grinning. "Personally, I'd rather save my strength for the awards ceremony." He leered, waggling his eyebrows.

"Uncle." He lowered his mouth to hers, catching her laughter.

* * * * *

▼™ SILHOUETTE
SPECIAL EDITION®
COMING NEXT MONTH

TEMPORARY DADDY Jennifer Mikels

That's My Baby!

Marriage, let alone fatherhood, was never an option for bachelor Dylan Marek, which was why he had run a mile when he fell for Chelsea Huntsford. Now Chelsea was back with a baby boy. Could he be Dylan's?

HEART OF THE HUNTER Lindsay McKenna

Morgan's Mercenaries

Captain Reid Hunter had sacrificed a personal life for the sake of his military career, and no woman could penetrate his steely heart—until he met Dr Casey Morrow. His mission was to protect her, but was he the one in need of protection—from love?

A HERO FOR SOPHIE JONES Christine Rimmer

The Jones Gang

Revenge by seduction was Sinclair Riker's objective and Sophie Jones was his intended victim! But there was something about Sophie's sweet kisses that drove all thoughts of vengeance from Sin's mind. Could Sophie turn Sin into a saint?

A FAMILY KIND OF GUY Lisa Jackson

At eighteen Bliss Cawthorne had been determined to marry Mason Lafferty, but her father had intervened, and Mason married another. Ten years later Bliss is back, and Mason, now a single father, is not about to let her go again!

EVERY COWGIRL'S DREAM Arlene James

To inherit her family ranch, Kara Detmeyer had been set the challenge of her life. She had to drive a herd of cattle hundreds of miles, *and* she had to do it with Rye Wagner, the moodiest, most gorgeous man she'd ever met.

DIAGNOSIS: DADDY Jule McBride

Big Apple Babies

Francesca Luccetti had a problem because, although she desperately wanted a baby, she neither had, nor wanted, a husband! An adoption agency seemed the answer—but the agency's handsome doctor, 'Doc' Holiday, had other ideas…

COMING NEXT MONTH FROM

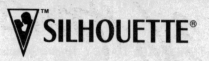

Intrigue
Danger, deception and desire

NEVER CRY WOLF Patricia Rosemoor
ONLY A MEMORY AWAY Madeline St. Claire
REMEMBER MY TOUCH Gayle Wilson
PRIORITY MALE Susan Kearney

Desire
Provocative, sensual love stories

A MONTANA MAN Jackie Merritt
THE PATERNITY FACTOR Caroline Cross
HIS SEDUCTIVE REVENGE Susan Crosby
THE RESTLESS VIRGIN Peggy Moreland
THE LITTLEST MARINE Maureen Child
SEDUCTION OF THE RELUCTANT BRIDE Barbara McCauley

Sensation
A thrilling mix of passion, adventure and drama

A PERFECT HERO Paula Detmer Riggs
IF A MAN ANSWERS Merline Lovelace
AN INNOCENT MAN Margaret Watson
NOT WITHOUT RISK Suzanne Brockmann

FREE!

4 Books
and a surprise gift!

We would like to take this opportunity to thank you for reading this Silhouette® book by offering you the chance to take FOUR more specially selected titles from the Special Edition™ series absolutely FREE! We're also making this offer to introduce you to the benefits of the Reader Service™—

- ★ FREE home delivery
- ★ FREE gifts and competitions
- ★ FREE monthly Newsletter
- ★ Books available before they're in the shops
- ★ Exclusive Reader Service discounts

Accepting these FREE books and gift places you under no obligation to buy; you may cancel at any time, even after receiving your free shipment. Simply complete your details below and return the entire page to the address below. *You don't even need a stamp!*

YES! Please send me 4 free Special Edition books and a surprise gift. I understand that unless you hear from me, I will receive 6 superb new titles every month for just £2.70 each, postage and packing free. I am under no obligation to purchase any books and may cancel my subscription at any time. The free books and gift will be mine to keep in any case.

E9EB

Ms/Mrs/Miss/Mr ....Initials...

BLOCK CAPITALS PLEASE

Surname...

Address...

....

....Postcode ....

Send this whole page to:
THE READER SERVICE, FREEPOST CN81, CROYDON, CR9 3WZ
(Eire readers please send coupon to: P.O. BOX 4546, DUBLIN 24.)

HELEN R. MYERS

Come Sundown

In the steamy heat of Parish, Mississippi,
there is a new chief of police. Ben Rader
is here to shape up the department, and
first on the list is the investigation of a
mysterious death.

But things are
not what they
appear to be.
Come Sundown
things change in
Parish...

MIRA®   **Available from 23rd April**